DEAD MAN DREAMING

Dead Man Dreaming

A novel

by

UDAY MUKERJI

Adelaide Books
New York / Lisbon
2019

DEAD MAN DREAMING
A novel
By Uday Mukerji

Copyright © by Uday Mukerji
Cover design © 2019 Adelaide Books

Published by Adelaide Books, New York / Lisbon
adelaidebooks.org

Editor-in-Chief
Stevan V. Nikolic

For any information, please address Adelaide Books
at info@adelaidebooks.org
or write to:
Adelaide Books
244 Fifth Ave. Suite D27
New York, NY, 10001

ISBN-10: 1-951214-46-3
ISBN-13: 978-1-951214-46-3

Printed in the United States of America

Chapter 1

Tack-tap, tack-tap, tack-tap—the sound of my own footsteps pricked me in the ears as I walked the long and empty corridor, echoing one end to the other. Perhaps wearing the leather shoes was a bad idea; I had never felt comfortable walking, making a statement. But Chloe had insisted. "Damn it," she had said, "it's your final year viva, so you must look professional." I hadn't had the heart to go against her wishes.

I took a quick glance at my watch. It was almost a half past twelve on a bright sunny afternoon, yet there wasn't a shred of daylight in the hallway. It always looked the same—day or night—under bright fluorescent lights. I looked around, but I saw nobody. Not many people were taking that corridor, anyway. Most patients and the hospital staff used the main entrance to the hospital. Supposedly, the management had built the walkway later to connect the university to the hospital for easy access to its doctors and students. And on that day, the authorities had also suspended most of the classes due to our exam schedule.

To take my mind off the ridiculous clickety-clack from my shoes, I tried to focus on the huge pictures on both sides of the wall. We had seen those pictures a thousand times in our residency days, and they always inspired us. The images captured the proud moments that created history in our hospital. We called that corridor our glorious "Hall of Fame."

As the hallway swerved to the right, I saw the room B16 on my left. My heart pounded like a jackhammer, but I marched on to reach the last threshold of my childhood dream. I had been waiting for this moment all my life. I felt so close to my dream I could almost smell my own operating room. While most people hated the typical iodoform smell in a hospital, I lived and thrived in that. I had waited all my life to be a heart surgeon.

I pushed open the thick wooden door, and I saw Dr. Tyler and three new faces sitting at a huge table in an otherwise bare and empty room. They were all sitting on one side, leaving one empty chair on the opposite side of the table. I immediately realized the handholding days were over. From that day on, I would be responsible for every call I made. I could be the messiah to bring hugs and kisses to the agonized and anguished families, waiting in corridors and in the waiting hall, and on the flipside, I would be answerable if anything went wrong in my operating room.

"May I come in, sir?" I asked as I entered the room. Dr. Tyler, our head of the department, introduced me to three other doctors from the medical board. But as soon as the introductions were over, it was as though someone had lifted a veil from my eyes, and suddenly, the final barrier didn't seem as scary as I'd thought. One by one—Dr. Tyler, Dr. Fisher, and Dr. Miller—they all asked questions, and I answered them all. The truth flashed before my eyes: if I couldn't breeze through the interview, I wasn't fit to be a heart surgeon. I didn't want to be the guy who would say "sorry" to the grief-stricken, worried families; I wanted to bring smiles to the waiting friends and relatives of my patients. I would rather accept failure there in that interview room than fail them at an operation table later.

I had always considered an operating room as the most sacred place on earth, where the distance between life and death often came closer than a nanometer. There's no room for leeway and no margin of error, so I had to know everything. A long time ago, I had also realized there was no easy or routine procedure. Every time, when a doctor cut open a human heart, they would come face-to-face with one of the world's finest creations. Any restoration work there needed knowledge, precision, and discipline. On top of all that, I would also need an understanding of the creator himself. I was sure no one would dare to restore Mona Lisa without trying to understand Da Vinci first.

A sudden jolt at my right hand brought me back to reality as Dr. Miller shook my hands and said, "Well, we got everything we needed. Wish you the best, David."

I looked at the big wall clock. One and a half hours had just passed in a flash.

"Thank you, sir." I stood up from my chair. Thank god it was over. But as I turned, the damn shoes got caught in-between the chair and the table, and I lost my balance. But I quickly grabbed one end of the table in front and saved myself from an embarrassing situation.

"Sorry about that, sir," I apologized.

"There's nothing to apologize for, son," comforted Dr. Tyler.

But as I made a move again to get out of the room, Dr. Fisher said, "I've one more question though."

I stopped, looked him in the eye, and tried to sound as confident as possible. "Sure, sir."

"Do you have Huntington's disease, David?"

Excuse me, that's none of your business, I wanted to say out loud. *Isn't that something personal?* But instead, I recollected myself and answered, "Not that I know of, sir."

"But given your family history, you know you have a fifty/fifty chance of getting it, right?"

My father had died of that disease sixteen years ago, and there was every possibility I was carrying it too. Anyone could draw that conclusion from my files. I looked at Dr. Fisher again and answered curtly, "Yes, I do, sir,"

"Have you got tested?" asked Dr. Miller.

"No, sir."

"Why not? Don't you want to know whether you have the disease or not?"

"No, sir, I don't. What's the point in knowing that, this point onward, my journey in life can only go down and can never go up? And there's no cure either to stop the damn disease until I'm dead. I think I'm better off not knowing."

"I understand your sentiment, son," Dr. Tyler said. "But here's the problem: knowing what we know from your file, we can't turn a blind eye…we must inform the board." He paused, then stood up, and took my right hand. "You've been a great student, David. And let me assure you that our present conversation doesn't affect your final score in any way. But the test is important if you want to work as a heart surgeon. You know how some surgeries can take hours, and a surgery can't be compromised by any lapses on the surgeon's part. However, you can always take a genetic test; that'll give us a better picture."

But at that point, I wasn't listening to him anymore. I didn't want to think about any of that. I pushed the chair with my right leg to make more space. Yes, I might have HD or not. So what? They'd no right to put me on the spot like that. I felt dizzy; I shook hands with Dr. Tyler and the rest, and I left the room.

As I stepped out, I saw Jolene sitting on a bench close to the door, waiting for her turn. She smiled and said, "Hi!"

My interview had overrun. But I was in no mood to explain "why." By rights, it should be their job and not mine. I said, "Good luck, Jo," and I walked off.

My heart was hammering hard in my chest; I feared it might explode anytime. Suddenly, my head went numb, my mouth dried up, and I felt as if the walls were closing in. But before I knew it, I was kicking a trash can that was sitting on one side of the wall in the hallway. It tumbled and rolled a couple of times on the floor, spilling everything from blood-soaked cotton balls, disposable coffee cups, and empty soda cans to leftover foods. I stood there for a moment, breathing hard and fast. I looked at the splattered trash on the floor, then walked through the garbage, stomping on everything that came under my fancy shoes. It wasn't a pretty sight, and I soon realized I'd made a mistake. I had to get myself out of that hospital before anything more embarrassing happened. I somehow dragged my six-foot corpse out of the main building and threw myself into the car.

I don't know how long I sat there, but must have been long enough. The carpark attendant noticed me in the CC camera and came to knock on my window. "Is everything all right, sir?" asked the attendant.

I quickly collected myself, rolled down the window, and answered, trying to read his name tag. "Sure, it's cool, Mike. I've been waiting for someone." I looked at my watch; it was almost a quarter past three. "Well, gotta go now . . . thanks, anyway."

I reached into my pocket to grab my phone. I wanted to call Chloe before going to her place, but I hadn't turned my phone back on after the interview was over. There were five missed calls and six messages in the last two-and-a-half hours—most of them were from Chloe, though one missed call was from my mother. *Both of them must have been waiting to know how I did at the interview. What am I supposed to tell them now?* Although Dr. Tyler said all this had nothing to do with my final result, I realized the job I had been eyeing for so long would be at risk.

The interview room in the hospital flashed before my eyes again. I quickly drove out of the carpark and called Chloe.

"Finally! What happened to you?" she asked in a worried voice.

"Nothing. What are you doing? We need to talk."

"Is everything all right, David?"

"Sure. Everything is fine. I'll pick you up at four." And I hung up. I felt a lump in my throat, and my voice was choking. I didn't want her to second-guess anything.

The drive from the hospital to Chloe's house at Bridgeland wouldn't take over fifteen minutes, but I wanted to take the edge off my turbulent mind before seeing her. I was still re-covering from the shock. I didn't want to appear before Chloe in that condition. I looked at my watch again and was glad I'd another half an hour to myself. As I got off the AB 1 and turned into Russet Road, I pulled up by the roadside.

"Have you got tested?" One question shook my whole world that afternoon, and it had been ringing in my head ever since. The question seemed unfair to me. They had no right to corner me with such personal matters.

More importantly, why question now? Did they expect me to be HD positive? That year, our hospital was going to re-cruit one heart surgeon from our department, and we were all eyeing the same position. But if they had someone else in mind, why this charade? Was this some kind of ploy to make me look unfit for the job? I could find a job in some other hospital, although I would've loved to work at Christchurch.

But I guess that chapter is now closed forever. I flung open the door, got out, and slammed it hard behind me. I looked up at the open sky and breathed.

Outside, the air was cool and crisp. I paced up and down in front of my car. *That question shouldn't have been a surprise to me; why didn't I see that coming?* There was always a good chance that I might have the disease. As Dr. Tyler had said, a surgeon's job required both skill and precision, so, it was understandable that a medical student must go through rigorous tests of many kinds before we could call them a heart surgeon.

Besides, I knew Dr. Tyler too well to think of the whole thing as some kind of ploy to undermine my credibility. I was sure he wouldn't do that to me. If I weren't good enough, he would've told me so.

Maybe what Dr. Fisher had asked was a little unusual for any normal student. But given my family history, I shouldn't be surprised. Any employer must have the right to know whether an applicant is fit for the work. Then, why was I fretting?

A fitness test for a new job was nothing new. Many professions required their applicants to meet the minimum physical standards regularly. Pilots in the aviation industry went through routine physical tests, including their visual acuity, color, and peripheral vision. The aspiring firefighters had to complete a series of tasks within a specific time, wearing a fifty-pound vest. They weren't complaining. A complicated heart surgery might take hours; physical strength with cognitive power and utmost coordination was vital to its success. And naturally, the board couldn't, or rather, shouldn't compromise with that. I guess, under the circumstances, only a pre-symptomatic test could prove my fitness. Huntington's chorea is a genetic disease. I understood their concerns, but it was still upsetting.

I grew up knowing I might succumb to that disease one day, but I never thought it would also stand in the way of achieving my dream to become a heart surgeon. Had I studied medicine for nothing? I wish they had told me about this fitness test the day when I got my admission into the medical college. Why didn't they? *Whose fault is it now? If I can't be a heart surgeon, what else can I do?* I had never prepared myself for anything else. I had invested all my time and energy into being a doctor. *How can I let all that go to waste now? How am I going to pay back my student loans?*

But as I came back inside the car and started the ignition, the dashboard clock in front reminded me of an even bigger problem at hand: *how do I break the news to Chloe?* Like all young couples, we also had made plans. What would happen to those plans? And with that thought, Chloe's smiling face popped up in front of my eyes. She had a beautiful smile— sweet and genuine with a tinge of girly shyness. But what could I say to her? The news would break her heart.

The traffic light in front turned amber and then red. I stopped, and I realized my reflexes were just fine. I was able to process my thoughts as any normal driver would. Maybe I was over-thinking the whole thing. Indeed, until I took the test, nothing would change. Perhaps I should hold off until then. Chloe knew my father had died of Huntington's chorea, and as a first-year resident physician, I was sure she knew what that meant.

At the turn of the road, I spotted Chloe on the upstairs balcony, despite the distance. She was ready in her regular denim shorts and a white tank top. She waved, and in the blink of an eye, she vanished to rush down the stairs.

Meeting Chloe three years before had brought a refreshing change to my life. I had met her in my first-year residency

at the Christchurch Hospital while she was doing her sophomore year in the medical school at the university. The first
time we met, she had no makeup on. She was wearing a pair
of jeans and a pullover. Chloe was no looker—average height
with medium built—but her intelligent eyes from behind the
oval glasses were deeply penetrating. She had big brown eyes
and piercing looks. After meeting her, for the first time in my
life, I felt an urge to connect with someone. She had natural,
well-defined arched eyebrows. She didn't wear mascara or eye-
liner every day like the other girls did, but when she did use
it, the makeup made her eyes look even bigger, though, in her
words, "a little twitchy." I had told her the fluttering eyes made
her look very sexy, but she just smiled.

"Hi! How did it go?" she asked as she opened the car door.

"It was great…" I paused, and we drove off. I wasn't sure
whether that was the time or the place to drop the bomb on
her.

"But…?" She waited for my answer. I guess she knew me
too well.

"No, there's no 'but.'" I tried my best to avoid getting into
that conversation. I was waiting for the right time. This might
change everything.

"I'm sure there is one. Otherwise, why did you pause?"

"No, I didn't pause; I stopped there," I said.

"But that sounded more like a pause to me." And she
looked at my face, waiting for my answer.

"You know I don't come from a family of native English
speakers, right? I guess that was my mistake." I tried to lighten
up the mood.

But Chloe's face turned pale, and she became serious.
"You can't always play the Indian card only to your advantage.
You're born and brought up here, so your argument makes no

sense. Anyway, if you don't want to tell me, why don't you say so?" She paused, looked out the window, and said, "Never mind, consider this the end of the conversation."

But what's the point in fighting over delivering some bad news? I have to tell her sooner or later, so why create a stupid misunderstanding? I looked out and noticed a café on the right side of the road, and I abruptly swerved and pulled over.

Chloe screamed. "Whoa, whoa, whoa! What're you doing?"

I soon realized my mistake; I could've caused an accident. But I was in no mood for an apology. Instead, I remained calm and asked her, "Want to grab a cup of coffee?"

"Sure. But what's all this?"

I looked into her eyes and said, "There is a 'but.' Now, you want to hear it or not?"

She didn't say another word. We got out of the car and found a table outside the café. After we ordered our drinks, she asked, "So? What happened there? Tell me everything."

I didn't want to sugar-coat anything. I said, "I might not get the heart surgeon's position in the hospital."

Chloe's eyes popped open. "What're you talking about? You're the best student they have this year. What happened? Did you not answer their questions?"

"Yes, I did . . . better than I had expected."

"Then, what's the problem?"

"My condition, my disease." And I looked away.

"What disease? What're you talking about?" She pushed aside the glass of water and the serviette stand to one side of the table and continued. "You're kidding, right?"

"No, I'm not kidding. It's Huntington's chorea," I replied calmly.

She looked at me and asked, "And since when do you have HD?"

"I don't know, at least, not yet."

Chloe looked impatient. "Could you please tell me what happened in there? You're killing me with all this nonsense."

I then narrated everything that Dr. Miller and Dr. Tyler had told me.

Chloe didn't know Dr. Miller, but she knew who Dr. Tyler was because she was doing her residency in the same hospital, so she grasped the gravity of the situation. Suddenly, we were both lost for words. The waiter came and served our drinks. Chloe's lips quivered; her eyes welled up and became red. She looked away to hide her expressions. I didn't know what she was thinking. I said, "For heaven's sake, say something, Chloe."

"But how do they know this?" she asked after a while, with her gaze still on the empty street. But when she had turned her face for a quick second, I saw tears at the corner of her eyes.

"Know what?"

She looked me in the eye and continued. "That you have Huntington's disease?"

"They know nothing for sure yet. Since my dad had it, Dr. Tyler wants me to take a genetic test; otherwise, they'll report to the medical board."

"That sounds unfair. Can they do that?" Chloe asked in a broken voice.

"I don't know. I guess they can; physical fitness can be a part of many eligibility tests."

"Can't we sue them for discrimination?"

"Sure, it's an option if they don't take me for my HD, but no one has said so, at least, not yet. Maybe they're just being cautious. Cautious is good, right?"

"How come?" Chloe was getting angry and impatient. That was unlike her, but I couldn't blame her. The board's demand was unfair. We both sat there speechless.

We had always considered ourselves mature, responsible, and educated members of society, so why we were seeing stars in broad daylight? Nothing made sense anymore. Our whole world was about to crumble in front of our eyes, and we couldn't do a thing. I clenched my fists under the table in frustration, but I was trying to control an outburst. I remembered what my mother used to say when I was a child. "Anger is a slippery slope." I couldn't let Chloe go down that path.

I looked at her and said, "My HD isn't confirmed yet, so let's take my case out of the equation for now. Still, how can a hospital allow anyone with HD to take chances on innocent patients' lives, knowing full well the surgeon can succumb to the disease any day?"

Chloe didn't answer. She kept quiet for a long time. I wasn't sure whether she was listening. After some time, I gave up, and I looked away at the horizon at the end of the road. The late afternoon sun threw long shadows on the street. A while later, I said, "Shall we? My mom will be eager to know what happened."

"Sure." She got up and moved to the car. I had no way of knowing what was going on inside her head. However, before I dropped her off, she asked, "Are you going to take the test?"

"I don't know yet. I'll call you later." And I drove off.

Ten minutes later, I reached my mom's house. We both lived at Erin Woods Boulevard, a quiet neighborhood in Calgary. We were only a few blocks away from each other. But I lived at the other end of the street, where a recent redevelopment had witnessed a few old houses giving way to new four-story tower blocks.

As I had expected, my mother had been waiting for me since the early afternoon. She was a busy woman. She never came home early from her office unless there was an emergency.

But this was something important to both of us. She too had sacrificed a lot for my career.

My parents had moved to Canada after my father got his medical degree in India and had married my mother. My father's parents were already in Canada, and my grandfather had been working for an oil company in Fort McMurray. So, moving to Canada had looked like a good opportunity for them.

My father knew he wouldn't be able to practice medicine in Canada with just his degree from India. He was told that all he had to do was take a few tests, which didn't bother him much because he had aced all his exams throughout his whole life. He had always been a merit scholar in India.

But the reality on the ground here was very different. The Canadian hospitals had to provide residency for their own medical students first; there weren't enough positions for the doctors with a foreign degree. Even after being in Canada for four years, my father wasn't able to practice medicine, and without a steady job, my parents faced major financial problems. So he'd sought an alternative career as a paramedic. The pay was just enough to get by, but they hadn't come to Canada to get by. They could've done that in India, with less stress. And it was about that time my mother started looking for a job.

My mother was an extraordinary woman—smart, intelligent, and soft-spoken. On top of everything, she was an artist and a good one too. She had been working in an ad agency as an art director until the day she got married. Like most Indian women, she'd also embraced her husband's future as her own and had sacrificed her career until the financial troubles hit them. Still, getting a job in a foreign country after almost eight years of hiatus scared her a bit at first. Nevertheless, she soon overcame the fear and clinched a job at one of the top ten agencies in Canada—a position she immediately declined, as the offer required her to move to Toronto.

Instead, she'd settled for a job in a smaller ad agency in Calgary. Soon, her career took off, but when she was offered a promotion, she again had to turn that down, as the assignment needed her to fly in and out of Calgary a few times a month. Thus, she remained in the same position as an art director in the agency. Despite the setbacks, she had never complained.

I was only a kid when all that had happened. She later told me why she had to sacrifice the promotion. My father had just been diagnosed with HD, and his condition deteriorated much faster than the doctors had predicted. He had needed twenty-four hours' attention and care. In spite of having attending nurses, my mother still had a lot to do at home. She felt she hadn't had a choice; with much irregularities, she was lucky to hold onto that job and the salary it paid, which became crucial to their survival.

After my dad passed away, maybe she could've tried to move up the corporate ladder again, but she worried her absence might affect my education. Besides, there was no one in the family to help if she had to leave town. My grandparents were living four hundred miles away.

As I parked the car and walked across the driveway, I saw my mother sitting on the front porch with a cup of coffee and her sketchbook. Most people watched television or listened to music to relax, but drawing was my mother's favorite pastime. My mother and her sketchbook were kind of inseparable. Sitting with her back to the street to enjoy the afternoon sun, she couldn't see me coming. I asked, "Hi, Mom, what are you drawing?"

"Just doing some sketches . . . So, how did it go? Do you want coffee?"

"No thanks, Mom. I'm good. Just had coffee with Chloe." Then I told her what had happened in the interview.

After hearing everything she kept quiet for a while and said, "I'm sorry, David."

"No, please don't do that. It's not your fault." I didn't want my mother to feel bad. The threat of the disease was already a jolt to her.

"Of course, it is; parents are always responsible for hereditary genetic diseases. I can't believe I was so ignorant. We should've done genetic testing," my mother said. "Anyway, let's do your test first before we jump to any conclusions. Do you want me to go with you? Or you can take Chloe along."

"No, Mom, I want to do this myself. Besides, I don't want to bother Chloe with this." Although my mother asked me to stay for dinner, I felt tired, and I politely declined. I said bye to her, and I left.

I had a lot on my mind, and I was dying to be alone. I wanted to go through the whole interview again. Why did they ask me about HD? Would they have asked me the same question if I hadn't tripped? Could I have avoided the situation, or would they have asked me anyway?

One question at the interview had changed my life within a couple of hours. Earlier, Chloe had behaved like she was upset, but she wasn't the only one. If the test came back positive, all our plans would fall apart. *Will they really push for the test? What will happen if I test positive? Will they still offer me the job?*

I simply couldn't think anymore. When I reached home, I opened the door and slammed it hard behind me. The loud thud that followed didn't bother me. All I wanted at that point in time was to shut myself in and think.

Three months before, I had asked Chloe one day, "Why don't you move in with me? You practically live here." She had said, "Sure, I don't see why not?" But she also had pointed out she didn't like the way I had asked. "Can you be any more unromantic?"

And ever since, we had been moving toward making that a reality. My present apartment being too small, we were looking for a new place. Since I had been busy with my exam, Chloe kept in close touch with the brokers. Although we confirmed nothing yet, she said she had the interior all planned out.

At first, Chloe didn't understand why I wanted to delay her moving in with me until my exam was over. When I told her I didn't want any distractions right before my final exam, she'd flared up, "So all I am is a distraction to you? Never mind, I don't want to move in with you."

I had tried to defuse the situation. "Isn't that a good thing? How am I going to concentrate if whenever I open my eyes, I only see you?"

"Okay, okay, I take it back. I don't want to distract you from your studies right now." Chloe had retracted her complaint without further arguments.

So what would happen to all those plans, to those houses we had seen—to those moments that would now look so ridiculously silly and meaningless? If the test result came back positive, that would practically seal my fate, irrespective of the job offer. Even if they did offer me the job, how long could I work? Financial problems aside, the HD onset would bring a whole set of new complications with deteriorating medical conditions.

I walked into the kitchen and pulled out a bottle of vodka I had in my pantry. I had never had a drink on my own before, so it had been just sitting there for more than a year. Besides, I had never liked the taste of vodka, having tried that once at a party. *But if it could bring relief to my immediate worries and anxiety, why not?* I took one quick swig; it tasted like shit and burned like hell. *Why do people drink?* I took a hard look at the bottle and thought, *there must be more to it.* So, I carried the bottle with me to the living room.

As I sat on the big couch, a picture of my dad on the console table caught my eye. My mother had brought that photo in her purse one day soon after I had moved into this apartment. The picture wasn't there because I loved him, but I also couldn't say I hated him. It was complicated.

The memories I had of my father weren't at all pleasant, except perhaps for one or two happy encounters, so I always avoided talking about him. Who knew, maybe I had blacked out most of my childhood memories to avoid thinking about him? We never had many father-and-son moments. I grew up seeing him bed-ridden. He had succumbed to the disease early. He never came to my hockey games or swimming competitions, and we hadn't played any board games at home as other families did. Most of the time, I played on my own, and sometimes our neighbor, "Uncle" Tom, joined me. Occasionally, I saw my dad's face through the window upstairs, sitting in his wheelchair and watching us play.

I could never figure out what to say to him. When I was much younger, he had often held me in his arms, and tears would roll down his cheeks, but he would say nothing. My mom later told me his speech got so impaired that he didn't want me to hear and remember him like that. He avoided me as much as I had avoided him.

Between her job, the domestic chores, and taking care of my dad, my mom had little time for me. At home, I was on my own. And before I knew it, my dad had passed away when I was only twelve years old. Since then, it had always been just me and my mother. My dad's prolonged illness and our financial instability had kept most of the relatives at bay. The only occasional visitors were my grandparents, although they had moved back to India after my father had died.

But what I hadn't known growing up was that the lack of friends and no active family life had had a silver lining too. It had given me a life free from distractions, and I concentrated on my studies. I had always been a straight-A student. My teachers had said I could study anything, but the helpless situation of my dad and my mother pushed me toward medicine. I wanted to be a doctor.

I gulped another drink and yet another. To my surprise, the afternoon's shock miraculously vanished and my worries subsided. I felt better—even slightly energized. I walked out to the balcony, still holding that bottle in my hand, and I looked at the night sky. It was a clear summer night: a yellow crescent moon was hanging on one side, and up above, there were only stars, stars, and more stars.

However, among those millions of flickering lights, I recognized Orion with his hunter's belt and sword. My dad had shown me that constellation when I was a kid. One evening, when I was in 4th grade, he had pointed his finger at a night sky, but at first, I didn't understand what he was trying to show me in the middle of a zillion stars. He had said, "See that constellation? That's Orion or the Hunter. Do you see it?"

"I see lots of stars, Dad." I was really puzzled.

Then he had drawn a few stars on a piece of paper and joined them one by one to form an outline of The Hunter. "The stars are in the same positions as I have drawn here; now imagine the lines."

He had then pointed his forefinger to the same constellation again and said, "See, those three dazzling stars slightly tilted? That's the hunter's belt, and you can spot it from anywhere on earth." He also showed me the stars that formed his shoulders and his legs. The Hunter was holding a shield in one hand and was carrying a club or sword in another, just as my dad had drawn on that piece of paper.

Almost twenty years later, I felt Orion still remained a strong connection between the two of us. Memories—which I thought had been buried a long time ago—came out gushing. I don't even remember how long I sat there watching the night sky with that vodka bottle by my side or when I finally went to bed that night.

The next day, when I woke up with a severe headache in the morning, I promised myself, "Never again." What had I been thinking? My head was as heavy as an iron ball, and my mouth was running out of saliva. I drank more water, went to pee, came back to my room and realized I was in no shape to start the day yet. I pulled back the curtains and curled into my bed again.

Moments later, I heard my phone ringing. But why was it so quiet? I was more inclined to believe I was dreaming rather than going through the whole reality check one more time. I sighed in relief as it stopped. But soon it came back on. This time, I followed the faint sound under my duvet and found the phone under a pillow. I always kept it in-between the two pillows on my bed. Had I pushed it underneath the pillow in my sleep?

I squinted to see the caller's name on the screen. Realizing it was Chloe, I cleared my throat and tried to sound as normal as I could. "Hey, good morning." But my voice sounded miserable even to my own ears.

"It's well in the afternoon, sir. Are you still in bed? Are you okay?" There came a barrage of questions. I wanted to tell her everything—but not yet. I still needed time to put my thoughts together, but I also knew I couldn't ignore her after turning the whole world upside down the previous evening. Inside, she must be freaking out.

"Don't worry about it. I went to sleep late last night. And as you know, I'm not rushing for anything now. I'll drop by later in the evening."

Chloe hung up, and I was glad I had found a peaceful middle-ground. I didn't know why, but I wanted to be alone. I didn't feel like talking to anyone. The silence was more comforting. At first, I wanted to go back to sleep, so I pulled the duvet up over my head and closed my eyes again. But I soon realized that, given the host of uncertainties surrounding my future, a sound sleep would be impossible.

Just a few days before, my life had been almost perfect, with a loving girlfriend and a bright career prospect. In the last twenty-four hours, it had become a total mess. *If the medical board doesn't approve of my being a heart surgeon, what else can I do?* I had never thought I needed a fallback plan. I had put all my time and energy on one thing only: being a good heart surgeon. If I couldn't do that, and I had to start over, where would I begin?

But lying in bed the whole day would also solve nothing. I got out, made a cup of coffee, and dragged myself to the living room. As I sat on the couch, Chloe's picture on the table smiled at me. She looked beautiful in that photograph. Her whole face lit up as she smiled. She had an amazing purity and simplicity written all over her face. How could I take that smile away? I couldn't let her down. That wouldn't be fair. *I gotta find a way out.* If I couldn't be a heart surgeon, there must be other things I could do to earn a living. Maybe I could take up research or teaching, but I knew it wouldn't be the same.

I got up from the sofa and walked to the balcony. It was a lazy Saturday morning. The rays of sunlight pierced through the maple leaves on our driveway. Dry leaves had fallen all over—on the empty street in front of the apartment building, on the driveway, and on my car. There was a kaleidoscope of colors: crispy brown, red, yellow and orange. As the gentle breeze swayed the branches, more leaves fell to the ground. Every time the wind blew, the fallen leaves on the street rolled on each other, kissing, hugging, laughing, and shushing. The leaves were dancing on the street like they owned the floor, rolling from the east to the west, and in the next minute, with the wind changing its direction, they trotted from the west to the east. And failing to resist the temptation, more leaves from the tree jumped in to join in the fun.

But suddenly, a speeding car came from nowhere and brutally rolled over—crunching and crushing—everything that came near the gruesome, grisly tires. The dry leaves broke into a million pieces with soft crackling sounds. Those who saved themselves did so by moving far, far away from the center of the street and huddling together close to the sidewalk. The street looked bare and naked. I sat down in a rude shock. I felt their pain and agony—much the same as what I had felt the day before when the hospital had mowed down my dreams.

Chapter 2

When I met Chloe later that evening at her house, I hadn't known I was in for a big surprise. I had been worried that she would bring up the unfinished morning conversation again. Instead, she started the evening with a huge apology. "I'm sorry about the way I reacted last evening. I should've been more understanding. From now on, you have my unconditional support, no matter what."

"Why're you apologizing? You did nothing wrong." I tried to calm her down.

"No, I want to be a worthy girlfriend."

"You're plenty worthy. You're more than I could dream of."

"You really mean it?"

"Of course, I do." God knew I meant every word I said.

Once the whole apology thing was out of the way, Chloe pulled out the real surprise. "I have booked a table for two at The Park."

"But why? What are we celebrating?" I couldn't resist my curiosity. I was surprised, because I'd grown up knowing The Park had over-priced menus and was one of the ultimate destinations for special occasions.

"Nothing special. It's just a treat for your final exam," declared Chloe.

"A treat for what? My whole future still hangs on the balance of a stupid blood test. I don't know whether I'll even qualify for the job." I tossed my coat on her bed and walked to the window. What was she thinking? What made her think that a dark moment in my career could be a cause for celebration?

Chloe threw her purse on the writing table and came running toward me. Her smile disappeared, and her face turned pale. Most certainly, she hadn't expected such a bitter reaction from me. She looked me in the eye and said, "No, dear, it's nothing of that sort. I'm sure you aced the exam, and the results will prove it next week. Remember what Dr. Tyler said, the test has nothing to do with your score? I didn't want the board's decision about the job to get to us. Besides, there's no verdict yet, no one knows anything for sure like you said. There's still a fifty-fifty chance that you may not even have the disease, right? And tomorrow, if your test results show you can't be a heart surgeon, that'll be okay too. We'll deal with that. I'm sure you can do other things."

She paused, then came a step closer and continued. "I'm sorry, dear. Maybe I didn't think it through. Tell you what, I'll cancel the reservation now."

I kept quiet for a minute. *I can't take my frustrations out on her.* She was only trying to cheer me up and be a supportive girlfriend. I extended my left arm to hold her and said, "Well, why not? Let's go and have dinner."

Forty-five minutes later, we were both comfortably sitting and thoroughly enjoying our dinner at The Park as if nothing had happened. And at the end of the dinner, although I wanted to settle the bill, Chloe insisted. "I got this."

Chloe had told me before that her father always pampered her with generous allowances. Her mother had passed away a long time ago, and her father had brought her up with little family help, so he didn't always know what to do with a growing-up girl. But according to Chloe, he tried his best. Giving money was his way of showing a single parent's affection toward his daughter.

Still, I couldn't believe Chloe just spent so much money on a fancy dinner. I asked, "But what prompted the treat?"

"As usual, last night, when my father saw me upset, he gave me some money and asked me to go out with my friends. You see, I'm still left with seventy dollars. What can we do? Any suggestions?"

"I would say, save it. If I can't find another job, we might need it."

"Ha-ha, hilarious."

Chloe's dinner treat had turned out better than nice, though. She was right: we needed something to take our minds off that stupid test. Who knew what would happen tomorrow? We sure couldn't live in constant fear. An hour later, when I pulled up the car to drop Chloe off in front of her house, she whispered, "Get out of the car."

"Your dad will kill me if I step in at this hour," I warned her.

"Who said we're going in?"

"Then where are we going?" I looked at her with infinite curiosity.

She had already started walking even as she called back, "We're going for a walk. Are you coming or not?"

I understood her feelings. I also didn't want that night to end. I wanted to hold on to everything around me. Every minute seemed so precious. I wished I could hang on to the feeling forever and never had to let go. The questions raised at the interview had come as a stark reminder of the reality ahead of me. I couldn't ignore the possibility of my having HD—that would be my future, maybe a little closer than I earlier had thought. Still, there was nothing wrong in living a little between then and now, so I followed Chloe. "Hey, wait up."

In spite of Chloe's best efforts to cheer me up over the next few days, I couldn't bring myself to think of the future. When Chloe called me the next morning, I kind of snapped at her. She called me a few times after that, but I didn't pick up. I didn't know what to say. I felt as if everything was slipping through my fingers. *The seeds of our hopes and dreams aren't any different from the seeds of plants and trees. Behind every blooming flower, there's always someone's hard work and watchful eyes.* My heart ached every time I looked at my dwindling hopes of getting the heart surgeon's job at the hospital. It was moving further and further away from my reach. The seeds of my ambition that I had nurtured all my life were dead even before fruition. Every time the thought came to my mind, I closed my eyes in dismay.

I had never suffered from any sleep disorders before, nor had I experienced much time lapse between my head touching the pillow and my falling asleep at night. But for the last few days, every time I went to bed, I invariably woke up after an hour or so in a semi-conscious state of mind: half-asleep and half-awake. My eyes remained shut, yet I clearly saw everything as if it were playing out on a stage in front of my eyes. My body was lying flat on the bed—numb and dazed—but suddenly, a look-alike emerged out of my body and started walking. I didn't understand what was going on. My confusions led me to believe it was a dream. I tried to pinch myself to validate my state of mind, but I couldn't lift my hands. In fact, I couldn't move any parts of the body. In spite of my brain's heightened activities, most of my muscles went numb and paralyzed. The whole body was thick and heavy with sleep.

I felt desperate for an explanation. I was dying to know who had just popped out of my body. He was roaming around like he owned the place. He peeped out of the window, then walked to the kitchen, drank water, and as he was coming back toward the bed, in total darkness, he stumbled on a pile of books stacked next to the cabinet and fell on the floor. I remembered Chloe had told me not to keep the books there.

"Ouch." I woke up with a jolt and freaked out, perspiring on a chilly night. I touched my face to check whether there were any bruises. Nothing. Then what was that? Just a bad dream?

After two consecutive nights with nightmares like that, I was scared to death even at the thought of going to bed. The next day, I took a mild sedative. I was prepared to do anything to stop those hallucinations. It was damn scary. And thank god, the sedative worked.

The next morning, I woke to a surprise knock on my door. I lived a very predictable life, and I had very few guests coming to my apartment. *And who would visit me in the morning?* I rushed to the door and saw Chloe standing there. *What is she doing here?* I stood there speechless, almost blocking the entrance.

"May I come in?" asked Chloe.

"Sure." I invited her in, and then I asked, "What brings you by in the morning?"

"What else can I do? Why aren't you taking my calls? I haven't seen you for four days. What have you been doing? And why have you stopped shaving?"

I wished I could tell her the truth—all about my sleepless nights and the nightmares. I never liked hiding anything from her. But I didn't want to scare her any more than she already was. The last five…six days had been miserable for both of us.

Remembering that Sunday's incident, I felt bad. Maybe it was the depression talking, but still, that wasn't an excuse. Had I hurt her? She had only been trying to cheer me up and help me get through this difficult time. I said, "I'm sorry for the other day. I didn't mean it."

Chloe came closer, wrapped her arms around me, and whispered, "I know. I know. Anyway, remember, they have no confirmation until you take the test. There's still a possibility that all this is just a bad dream."

"I hope so too." And I held her tight.

After a few more sleepless nights and hours of deliberations— sometimes with Chloe and other times just myself—I returned to the hospital, eight days after my exam. When I reached Dr. Tyler's office, he behaved as if he was waiting for me. He got up from his chair and directed me to a sofa in the corner of his room. He said, "You're the person I was looking for. I was about to call you."

"You were?" I blurted out.

Dr. Tyler sat on the other empty sofa and said, "In fact, we had an internal meeting that day after you left. The hospital board has decided to offer you the position of a heart surgeon here. The medical board has agreed with us that you should practice even if you test positive in genetic tests, until such time as HD symptoms surface."

I immediately thought of Chloe. She was right. I had panicked for nothing. I wanted to call her, but I also didn't want to look unprofessional. I thanked Dr. Tyler and asked, "Well, when do I start?"

"Don't forget, you still have to take the pre-symptomatic test," Dr. Tyler reminded me.

"Why? If the test means nothing…" I tried to reason with him, but he didn't even let me finish.

"It means a lot to the board, David."

"But what happens if I don't want to know?"

"We'll respect your decision; you have the final word on this. Even if you don't take the test, there're still many options before you. However, if you want to be a heart surgeon, the board feels they need to know the progress of the disease in case you have it. Since the test can't predict when the symptoms will begin and the course it will take, the best thing would be to monitor it on a regular basis," explained Dr. Tyler.

"Fair enough. Let's do the blood test. I'm ready."

"Are you sure? Have you discussed this with your family?"

In the last few days, Chloe and I had rarely talked, but whenever we did, all we talked about was this. My mother knew I would be taking the test, although she didn't know the exact date. But we all had realized that the test was vital to securing the job at the hospital, so I nodded.

"Let's go to the lab then."

Twenty minutes later, as we walked out of the lab, he grabbed my left shoulder and said, "Come by tomorrow morning for the test result. Bring a friend or family member if you like. I'll also schedule an appointment with our genetic counselor for you."

"Is that necessary?" I murmured.

Nothing seemed necessary at that point in time. Ever since that momentous interview had taken place, my life had been on a roller-coaster ride. One minute, everything looked normal, and the next minute, the world was falling apart. Minutes ago, Dr. Tyler had offered me the job I had been eyeing all my life, but it came with a caveat—the knowledge of possibly carrying a life-threatening HD.

My personal life too had been falling apart. I had been a wreck, hallucinating almost every night. I hadn't talked to my mother since I had told her about the outcome of the interview. She had called me a couple of times, but I didn't pick up. I wasn't in a mood to talk to anyone. But my interview had shaken her badly. When I tried calling her the day before, I got her voice mail. Now that I thought about it, I started worrying about her. Our last conversation hadn't ended all that well. I knew the guilty feeling had been eating her up, and I needed to talk to her.

My relationship with Chloe was also going through a rough patch. Although we were trying to act normal, I was slowly losing control. Chloe insisted it was nothing, but I couldn't ignore the possibility of an end of my career even before it had started. She had said, "It's a fifty-fifty chance," but what would happen if I ended up at the dark end of the fifty percent? How could I ignore that possibility? I was sure that Chloe was scared too, and she was just putting up a brave front. But for whom? Me? How long was she going to keep that up? The truth was, my future—our future—depended on that test. Maybe, the test wasn't a bad decision after all. A lot more than my career was riding on the test.

Chloe was a simple girl; all she ever wanted was a small family and a house in the suburb with picket fences and all that. Her definition of a small family had two kids and a dog, and all that was fine with me too until I got the wake-up call. My interview last week had forced me to re-assess my future. I had never believed in making empty promises, and in my present situation, I couldn't afford to think of years ahead of us anymore. Could I forget all about the possibility of my HD? After what had transpired, I couldn't even think of what would happen a month ahead of time, let alone marriage and kids. I couldn't bring another child into this world with any possibility of HD. That would be insane, but Chloe loved kids. She had even picked a gender-neutral name for our first child: Chris. She had said it could go either way, Christopher or Christina.

Nevertheless, I wanted to put everything on hold until I got the test results. And then I needed to have a long discussion with her. It wasn't just about the job anymore.

But our conversation that evening took an ugly turn. I had waited all day to break the news about the job offer with a dinner in the evening. I knew how much this would mean to her, but before I could say anything, Chloe told me she had fixed an appointment to go and see another house. I blurted out, "Can we do that next week?"

"Why put it off? I thought you wanted to move in together." She gave me a curious look.

"Sorry, I can't think about the future right now; my every day is a new battle," I retorted.

"I understand that. Trust me, I'm with you on this." Chloe expressed solidarity.

But there were also other things I needed her to consider. I said, "I know you want to help, but HD, if confirmed, is beyond anyone, Chloe."

"What's that supposed to mean? Is there something you aren't telling me?"

Chloe was right. I had something even bigger to discuss with her: the kids. But I wasn't sure whether it was the right time to talk about a decision that could change everything.

Besides, there was no point in discussing it before the test result was out. I didn't want to scare her. I looked at her and said, "Let's wait until I sort things out with the hospital. I want to make sure that we can make the rent every month."

But I also didn't want her to worry about our finances, so I said, "I got the job, Chloe. Although the board wants me to take the test, the result will have no impact on my practicing there."

"There you go." Chloe couldn't suppress her joy. "I told you Dr. Tyler wouldn't want to lose you to another hospital."

"Still, everything seems so uncertain now. Can we please wait?" I pleaded.

On other days that would've been the end of our conversation about the new house. But unfortunately, Chloe wasn't done. She asked, "So what's really stopping you from seeing the house? You know, this house may not be on the market for long."

"Don't worry. There'll be others."

"So, you're a psychic now?"

I looked at her face in shock; that was so unlike Chloe. But then, she had been behaving rather erratically for the last few days. In fact, we both had been behaving a little oddly. I could understand her feelings: she seemed to be trying to collect everything that was rightfully hers, lock them under her care, and stand guard at the gate. Naturally, the fight wasn't about the house anymore, and it would be disastrous if I told her my dilemma about having kids. To diffuse the tension I said, "No, Chloe, if not this one, we'll find another house. I promise. But right now, I can't really think about any of this. Please."

When we talk about something, meaning to talk about something else, it's always difficult to find a solution. Even if we danced around the house issue the whole night, we would've solved nothing. Our whole world had been turned upside down since that interview, so I couldn't blame her for feeling shaky; I was feeling a little insecure too. But I couldn't reassure Chloe of our relationship until I made my position clear about having children if I tested positive.

The next day, as I entered the hospital, I met Dr. Tyler in the lobby. He was about to head out, but he changed his direction as soon as he saw me. "Hi, David! How are you? Come with me," said Dr. Tyler in his usual, cheerful tone.

I had been feeling jittery all morning. I had hardly slept the night before. The test result was all that I could think about. I was trying to read Dr. Tyler's face for any clue, but there was nothing unusual in his behavior. *What does that mean? Am I in the clear? Or that he doesn't really know the outcome of the result either?*

He took me to the genetic counselor's office and said, "Meet Dr. Laura Bergmann. She'll take you through your report. I'll be back in my room in twenty; see me after you finish here."

I didn't understand why Dr. Tyler took me to a counselor. I was in no mood for a long prelude. *Goddamn it! I'm a doctor too. Give it to me straight,* I felt like telling him to his face. I wanted to get my report card and get out, but I didn't have the heart to tell him anything. I said, "Sure, sir."

Dr. Bergmann was an excellent counselor. I had heard about her in our residency days but never had the opportunity to meet her. She led me to a chamber and spent close to forty-five minutes in getting to know me. She asked me every detail about my family life, about my relatives, my mother, and my girlfriend. I was in no mood for any conversation, though; I was anxious to get my report. My heart was racing, but I answered her politely. Then, she handed over the report and said, "You can open it now if you like."

I took the envelope from her hand and opened it. Only one line stood out in that report: HD positive. Everything else looked hazy and blurry. I don't remember what I was thinking at that moment, but I wasn't listening to Dr. Bergmann. My eyes were still fixed on the report. Her face appeared a little blurred in my peripheral vision and her voice was very distant. I heard her saying, "The result doesn't say at what age the symptoms will appear or what those symptoms will be like. Besides, the symptoms vary from person to person, in progression and in severity. As you probably know, a positive test result doesn't mean you have any HD symptoms right now. A positive or high-risk result means that at some point in life, symptoms of HD will appear. And we all have to be prepared for that. Let's fight this thing as a team."

What does that even mean? All I heard was a lot of blah-blah-blah. To be honest, I wasn't paying any attention to her. How could I? How could my life be over so soon? I was only getting started. I was sure Dr. Bergmann was trying her best to cushion the fall for me, but that was beyond anybody; they had just declared my death sentence.

Soon, all confusions ended as Dr. Bergmann pushed her chair back and stood up. I felt relieved at the sign of the end of the session. She shook my hand and said, "Please call me if you have any questions. You know where to find me." And she smiled. She reached into her top left drawer for her name cards and passed me one for her contact numbers. And then, my very first HD counseling session was over.

Chapter 3

I slowly walked to Dr. Tyler's office, even though I wasn't in a mood to talk to anyone. It became clear from his expressions that he hadn't really seen the blood test report until I threw it on his desk. His usual smile was gone in a flash, and his face hardened. He blurted out, "I'm sorry, David." But he quickly collected himself and asked, "So, you're joining us next month? I'll get HR to send you the appointment letter, although you can join us earlier if you want to."

I thanked him for his support and walked out of the hospital, dazed, and sat on a bench in the small park just opposite the main building. My legs felt heavy, and they refused to walk any farther. My heart weighed down on me too. In an instant, my relationship with that hospital had changed forever. *They won't see me as a promising heart surgeon anymore—instead, another patient, waiting in line to die.*

The job I had been waiting for so long now looked meaningless. Whether anyone wanted to admit it or not, it was the beginning of an end for me. I had seen my father's health decaying day by day.

I shivered thinking about how Chloe and my mom would take the blow. *The confirmation of HD will kill them. We always believe in miracles when the odds are stacked up high against us.*

That's just human nature. I could bet they were both hanging on to the other end of the fifty-percent chance of my having HD. Maybe, secretly, I had been latching onto that hope, too. But now that the truth was in front of me, I had no idea what to do next. My mother had experienced living with an HD patient before, but Chloe would be totally new to such things. *Why bring her into all this? Why ruin her life too?* Besides, after the confirmation, I definitely wouldn't want to have kids. How could I expose an innocent child to such a deadly disease? That would be so irresponsible. Yet how could I deprive Chloe of the one thing she wanted so dearly in life?

Although I would've loved to spend the day alone in my apartment, I couldn't rest until I spoke with Chloe. We went for an early dinner to a Mexican restaurant close by.

"What did I do to deserve the treat?" she asked. "Did you get the test result?"

"Nope, not yet." I had never lied to her before, but that one was necessary. "I should get it in a day or two. Anyway, Dr. Tyler said I could start work next month."

"Thank god. That's great news. Now I get it. The treat is for the new job, right?"

"Yes, you're right, but I also have something important to discuss with you."

The confirmation of the job at the hospital had definitely lifted Chloe's mood. She looked at me and smiled, pushed her wine glass to one side, and asked, "What is it?"

"It's about us." I paused and hesitated for a minute. The busboy came and cleared the dinner plates, leaving the wine glasses. Until that point our life had always been simple, made of small wishes like sleeping in late on a Sunday morning or climbing into bed next to our loved one. I had been an obliging boyfriend, and she was an obliging girlfriend.

"Go ahead, I'm listening." Chloe sounded impatient.

"I don't know how to put it, and I also don't want to sugar-coat anything. So, I'll just say it—I don't want to have kids."

Chloe's jaw dropped as if the world was coming to an end. She looked disappointed and pale. She asked, "But…why? You know we won't be having kids anytime soon, right? Not at least in the next five to six years?"

"I know that, but I don't want to bring another person into this world with any possibility of carrying HD. As you know, the kids will always have a fifty/fifty chance of having the disease."

"But there's also a fifty/fifty chance of them not having it, right? Besides, having two kids doesn't mean that one of them must have it; each kid has a fifty/ fifty chance."

It would have been much easier for me to justify my stand if I could only tell her the truth, but that would crush her totally. Besides, she might feel duty-bound to stay with a dying boyfriend. I didn't want to put her on the spot.

Chloe was a resident physician. She knew what Huntington's disease meant. But of late, I noticed she had been reading more about HD than anything else. She asked, "Isn't our whole life is about taking chances?"

"That's different," I retorted.

Chloe looked me in the eye and asked, "Different, how?"

I wish I could tell her right away that I had had a fifty-fifty chance, too, and it turned out that wasn't good enough. I wanted no one to go through what I was going through. But I kept quiet for a while. I looked at her and said, "In life, we get a choice whether we want to take a chance or not. But in this case, we aren't leaving it up to the child. The child has no say in this matter."

"We also have very little say in many matters in our life. Accidents just happen. A moving bus can hit you or a tsunami can sweep you away. What do you have to say to that?"

"One thing: what are the odds? Besides, when the odds are high, we can take precautions like we do when we see a tornado coming, but in this case, there's nothing we can do. Anyway, I don't want to fight with you. I know how much you want to have kids, and I have no right to force my thoughts on you. I just wanted to let you know my decision."

"Well, what happens if the test comes back negative? At this stage, you're just panicking. Tell you what, if you want, we can fast-forward to the next chapter and get married and have kids now. We don't need to wait."

"But that isn't a solution, Chloe"

"Then what is?"

"I don't know. I don't have one. That's why my answer will still be the same."

"Now you're being stubborn."

"Call me stubborn or call me skeptical, after what I have gone through the last few days, I don't want anyone to face that. There're thousands of genetic diseases, and I'm too scared to be a parent in case I pass one on to my kids."

"Well, where does that leave us? You know that's just life. If your parents didn't have kids, I wouldn't have met you."

We were arguing with no solution in sight, but all I could think of was why let an innocent child be a part of this trauma? Besides, Chloe sure didn't sign-up for this as a girlfriend. And if she knew the test results, she might feel obligated to stay with me irrespective of this decision. I didn't want to push her into a situation where she would have to choose between having kids and sticking by a dying man. I said, "I admire your courage, Chloe. I know you're ready to face life head-on. But I'm afraid, after what has happened, I might not be ready in a long time. And maybe never. But I tell you what, we can always adopt."

"Why do I want to raise someone else's kid when I can have my own child—my own flesh and blood? It's not the same thing, you know." She paused, thought for a minute, and asked, "Well, how about gene editing?"

"Are you hearing yourself now? Gene editing isn't legal in this country or even in the US. But we can opt for sperm donation." I tried to suggest a viable alternative.

"You don't get it, do you? I want our kid; I want to have a child with you. If anything untoward happens, we'll deal with it. Who knows what God wants for us?"

"Please don't bring God into this."

"Why not? Now you don't believe in God?"

"I don't want to talk about God now. It has nothing to do with God. You believe in taking chances, and I don't."

"So, what does that mean for us?" Chloe asked.

I heard a loud thumping noise inside my chest, and my head started spinning. I said, "Maybe we should take a little time apart to think? I'm sure that won't change my position, but it doesn't mean you should change yours. You deserve to have kids, and I can't let you sacrifice that. Someday, you'll be a great mother. We both need time to think after all that has happened in the last few days. Shall we take a break?"

"Maybe we should. Now you're making no sense, and I can't deal with it anymore. If everyone starts to think like you, the world will come to an end in no time. Take all the time you need, but I'm not changing my mind, either. Call me again when you change yours." She picked up her bag and asked, "Will you drive me home now?"

When we reached her house, she quickly got out of the car and slammed the door shut. She looked back but said nothing. It was a lot for her to digest in one evening. Possibly, she was fuming inside. I had never seen her behaving that way, but we had to do it. She might be better off not knowing, and perhaps, she would be happier without me.

It felt like someone had amputated parts of my heart, but the breakup was inevitable. I loved her too much to deprive her of the one thing she had ever wanted. Besides, I didn't want to drag her into my imminent, lingering health problems. I shivered at imagining Chloe cleaning up after me for the rest of her life. I couldn't put her through that, but had I pushed her to the brink in the process? Otherwise, Chloe would've never reacted that way.

The next day, when I woke up, a picture of Chloe on the writing desk caught my attention. It immediately reminded me of what had happened the previous night, puncturing a new hole in my heart. I got up from the bed, took the picture, and shoved it in my cupboard. I dragged myself to the kitchen to make coffee. But as soon as I took the first sip, my favorite, big, black coffee cup reminded me of Chloe again. Knowing my obsession with coffee, she had bought me that huge cup as a birthday present the previous year, and ever since, it had reminded me of her every morning. I held it tight with both hands and took a hard look at the cup. Obviously, I didn't need that reminder every step of the way. I took out my old coffee mug from the cabinet and poured my coffee into that. I threw the black cup in the sink and thought maybe I could just keep it and not use it anymore. Who knew, but in the last three years, Chloe had left more fingerprints in that house and in my heart than I could ever imagine. But I wasn't ready to wipe them clean just yet; I only wanted to see them less.

I walked into the living room and sat on the couch, thinking I had the whole day ahead of me, but I had nothing to do and nowhere to go. Until about a week before, I had always had tons of things to do—I was always rushing. Between my crazy hospital shifts and studying for exams, I had very little time for house chores or even meeting Chloe. How come, within a few days, everything had just disappeared from my horizon?

Chances were, I would never be a great heart surgeon with this life-threatening disease hanging over my head. Even after I joined the hospital, my HD would haunt me every day for the rest of my life. My relationship of three years had also come to an end. Just the thought of all that made me shudder again. What did I do to deserve that?

But among all those depressing thoughts that morning, something good happened. I got a text message from the Medical Board: our final year results were out. I ran to my laptop to check my score, and then Jolene called. "Well, you did it again," she said. "You're now officially the topper of 2012."

I immediately thought I could use this piece of good news to tell my mother about the blood test result. After I got off with Jolene, I walked over to my mother's place as I needed to do this face-to-face.

When she heard I had come out on top she hugged me and said, "That's my boy. I knew it. Bring Chloe for dinner in the evening. We must celebrate."

"Chloe and I broke up, Mom."

"Why? When did that happen?" my mother asked.

"Just last night. You know how badly Chloe wanted to have kids, and I couldn't have kids in this condition," I explained.

"What condition? Have you done the test yet?" And she looked at me anxiously.

Then, I told her about the blood test report. But surprisingly, this time, my mother didn't go on a self-imposed guilt trip again like she had done when I first told her about the interview. She said in a solemn voice, "Let's take one day at a time, and let the future be always unknown."

"How is that possible? I already know my future, Ma."

"No, you don't. All you know is you have HD and you'll face problems at the onset of the disease. So? We all know we're going to die, but do we stop living?"

That was a good argument. If I had ten years, I wanted to spend those ten years living and not brooding. Knowing my break-up with Chloe made matters worse, a week later, my mother bought me a round-trip ticket to Italy. She knew Chloe and I had been planning to go there.

She said, "This is my gift for your final year result. Do this before you start work at the hospital next month. God knows when you'll have time for the next vacation."

"But…"

My mother interrupted me. "There's no 'but;' you need a vacation."

I said, "You want me to go to Italy by myself? That's ridiculous."

"No, it's not. Think about it: it's your opportunity to meet more people and familiarize yourself with the local culture. I should've sent you to Europe after you had finished high school. But you know how things were with us; I couldn't afford it then. Rome is beautiful and so are Florence and Venice. Trust me, you'll love it."

"I don't want to go to Venice alone, Mom."

"Why not? Venice has more to offer than its canals and romantic gondola rides. Go see how conviction and dedication can beat the odds. It's amazing how we always find solutions in adversities. If we can't stop a disaster from happening, we can still save ourselves by insulating us from the danger. And that's what the Venetians are doing."

The truth was, I needed no real convincing—I also wanted a break. I had to get away from the never-ending chaos in my head about Chloe. Old memories were chasing me like an addiction to drugs.

Perhaps travel could help with the ongoing nightmares too. Just two days before, I had woken up again in the middle of the night with another frightening dream. It was as vivid as a camera rolling in my living room. I saw myself in a pajama suit, sitting in a wheelchair trying to roll up to the window. But I couldn't figure out why I was wearing a pajama suit. I wasn't in a hospital; everything there looked the same as in my living room, of course, except the wheelchair. Also, I had never worn a pajama suit in my life; I was more used to boxer shorts. But every time, I tried to roll the chair forward, in spite of my best efforts, I couldn't even move an inch. I didn't have the strength to do so. To gain power, I took a deep breath and pushed the wheels one more time with all my strength. Still, nothing happened.

I banged my fists on the wheels in frustration. The tears came forth like water spilled from a bursting fountain. But why was I crying? I never cried before. The more I tried to stop the sobbing, the harder it came, punching my heart and ripping my veins and guts. I wanted to curl up in my wheelchair, but I couldn't pull my legs up. I heard footsteps; they came closer and closer. Was that the night nurse coming to check on me? But soon the sound died down. In my desperate attempt to get some attention, I called out, "Help! Help!" But I couldn't hear anybody. I called again, "Anybody?... Please." And I woke up to the sound of my own voice, with a damp and wet feeling on the left side of my face. It was that hallucination again, although the tears were real.

Remembering that nightmare, I quickly thanked my mother for the generous and thoughtful gift, and the next thing I knew, I was on a flight to Rome, on my first trip to Europe. I felt a little sad at first because Chloe and I had wanted to do Europe together, but I told myself again that breaking up was the only option. If I had spent more time with her, the break-up would've been only that much more difficult. I couldn't hide the report from her for long, and then she would've felt duty-bound to stay with me. I couldn't let that happen.

I loved Rome, I loved Florence, but I was lost for words the moment I reached Venice. I didn't want to miss anything, so, instead of flying, I took trains from Rome to Florence, and then on to Venice. An overwhelming new reality gripped me the moment I reached the train station in Venice—Venezia Santa Lucia. I had heard stories about Venice all my life and even read some travel sites, but nothing came close to experiencing the city up-close. For the first time in my life, I landed in a city surrounded by water and hundreds of tiny islands. I got out of the train station and headed for a water bus, locally called, "Vaporetto."

I stayed in a hotel at Giudecca Island —quiet, serene, and away from the tourist-infested Main Island where almost every other person was holding out their cell phones to capture a slice of Venice. My hotel was only ten minutes ferry ride away from the railway station, and the view from the hotel was amazing, overlooking the Giudecca Canal, a waterway much wider than the Main Canal. Gentle water, creating ripples, rolled toward the San Marco Basin all day long. The ripples kept changing colors from golden glitters in the sunshine to milky white on a full-moon night. I could also see the bustling central Venice and Saint Mark's Basilica from the opposite bank of the canal while sipping coffee in my room or at a roadside café. It was total silence in absolute serenity. I loved it, because it was every bit of Venice but the crowd.

Although my mother had said I should get to know the people there, I was in no mood for new friendships. I preferred solitary walks thinking about what my new life would be like, minus Chloe. She would've loved it there; she was always so romantic. I was also sure I would've enjoyed Venice much more if I wouldn't have missed her so much. But I also knew, it was what it was, and I needed to focus on the present.

I loved the slow, carefree pace of life in Venice. Maybe it seemed slow to me because I had nothing much to do there. Possibly, business was just great for the locals. Tourists were pouring in every day, traders were ferrying their goods, doctors were attending to their patients, and children were going to schools. The only difference was much of it happened on the water. Water boats were the main mode of transport there. Most houses sat just a few inches above the water level. And in spite of living with the constant fear of rising water levels, Venice retained its charm as one of the most beautiful places on earth.

Over the next few days, I spent hours walking along the narrow lanes, chasing the canals that ran through the islands. The long walks in Venice along the lanes and alleys surrounded by tiny canals opened my eyes. *How do they live in perpetual fear with the water level at their threshold every day? It's water everywhere, and the tiny islands are all connected by small footbridges.*

"How many islands do you have in Venice?" I asked Marco, the restaurant manager at the hotel.

Marco told me the city had one hundred and eighteen small islands, separated by one hundred and seventy-seven canals. And over four hundred bridges connected them back.

Venice had been sinking for a long time, but people there had refused to accept the obvious to be their fate. That's why they were building a massive wall—perfect flood barriers that could be raised at high tides—to protect the lagoon. *If they can insulate themselves from sinking under the sea, why can't we shield ourselves from genetic diseases? There's gotta be a way out.*

A week later, when I came back home, I became obsessed with the idea. And I had already made up my mind. When I reached the hospital, I went straight to Dr. Tyler's room, and he greeted me with a warm "Hello." But I didn't want to waste his time. I said, "I don't want to be a heart surgeon anymore."

He looked like he had seen a ghost. His face lost its color. He said, "Why David? I have made all the arrangements. The board leaves us in charge to monitor everything. They're out of your hair for good."

"No, it's not about them; I want to do something else."

"What do you want to do?" Dr. Tyler gave me a curious look. "I get what you're going through; please see Dr. Bergmann. I heard you already missed the last session."

"Sorry about that, sir, I went to Italy for a few days."

"That's great, David! Tell me more about the trip." He put his arms behind his head and pushed his chair farther away from the table, waiting for me to start.

"It was great, sir, but it also helped me see things from a new perspective."

"Then, what is it that pushed you away from surgery?" asked Dr. Tyler.

"Nothing pushed me away from anything, sir. I admit, the last few days, before going to Venice, I was praying hard to get this job in the hospital, but later I realized it wouldn't be fair to operate on patients with a death warrant hanging over my head. My imminent illness doesn't bother me as much as the fear of failing my patients in an operation room. That will be terrible, sir. Maybe Jolene or someone else would be a better fit."

"But…" Dr. Tyler was going to say something.

I interrupted him and continued. "I want to step aside. That's the right thing to do, sir. Besides, in the last few days, I have spent a lot of time thinking about my future. My genetic disease needn't be the end of it all—it can be the beginning of a new chapter. I want to channel my anger and frustration into finding a solution to all hereditary genetic diseases. After all, medical science has prevented tuberculosis and cholera, haven't they? In the limited time I have, what I really want is to build barriers for all hereditary genetic diseases. I have to stop it before it's transmitted."

"That's great thinking, David. But how are you going to achieve that?" he asked. He looked worried.

"Venice opened my eyes, sir. A few years ago, no one thought Venice could be saved from going under the sea in another two hundred years. But Venetians have done the impossible, or at least, they're near completion. They've built retractable gates protected by a string of flood barriers that can be raised at high tides. Once all these gates are in place, they'll be able to plug every single inlet when the water level rises in the Adriatic Sea."

"That's all good, David. We can draw inspiration from there. But as you know, all genetic conditions aren't inherited from parents. New mutations or changes in the DNA can also cause them. There are also multi-factorial disorders like diabetes and heart disease."

"I know all that, sir. We already studied that in our class. But I'm not just thinking about HD; there're thousands more genetic diseases passed down from parents to children. First, I want to work on single-gene diseases, and then we can look at other forms of genetic disorders."

"Well then, tell me how you're going to do that?" questioned Dr. Tyler.

"I am not sure yet, sir. I'm still struggling to get the right answer. I need time. But I also know I have to repay my student loans and earn money for my living expenses," I conceded.

Dr. Tyler looked confused. He leaned back in his chair again, maybe to consider the whole thing in the light of new developments. Then, he got up and walked up and down the length of the room a few times. I sat there, watching him and occasionally catching a glimpse of the day sky through the window. Then, he looked at me and said, "You can teach if you need a regular job to pay your bills. Or, I can try to find you a position in our R&D. But if you pursue that as a career, you should consider getting a Ph.D. You can get in now, but to run your own research team someday, you'll need a Ph.D."

I appreciated what he was trying to do, but I wasn't yet ready for a regular job. I had to give my idea some kind of a shape before I could take on something else. I knew building a physical barrier to stop the water flow was one thing and the idea of blocking genetic diseases from passing on to the next generation was quite another. I didn't want to lose focus with a full-time job, losing more time. Besides, I didn't even know how much time I had. I was sure Dr. Tyler didn't expect me to turn down that heart surgeon's job after he had convinced the board. I didn't want to put him in that kind of situation again. I knew he worried about me too. He was simply trying to pull me back into a routine again, but I wasn't ready to think about another job, at least, not yet. I said, "Thank you, sir. Can I think about it?"

At that stage, my imagination was running wild. I had no concrete plan to convince anyone. I had seen a ray of hope in Venice, but I couldn't put my finger on it. So, I wanted to pursue it.

"Of course. But are you sure you want to give up this surgeon's opportunity in the hospital? The board might not be willing to extend the same offer as time goes by," stressed Dr. Tyler.

"I thought about it, sir. I know what I want to do," I confirmed.

"Well, I wish you good luck, David. You're a bright and intelligent guy; I trust your intuition. Keep me posted."

Chapter 4

The next morning, when I woke up, I felt as if a huge weight had been lifted off my shoulders. The thought of putting my patients' lives in danger if my HD symptoms sneaked in without my knowledge was killing me. I didn't want to take that risk. The next person I needed to convince was my mother. I didn't want to keep her in the dark. Besides, Venice was her idea, and it all started there.

I looked at my watch. It was half past five in the morning. But I felt rested, and I didn't want to go back to sleep again. I walked to the balcony; there was a freshness in the air. My conversation with Dr. Tyler the previous day had set me free, but I couldn't ignore how much he must've fought for me. Although he had said nothing, I felt I had disappointed him. My only hope was, someday, I could make him proud of something even bigger. But I was glad all that had marked the end of a chapter for me. Here on, though unknown, it would be a whole new beginning.

When I reached my mother's place and picked up the newspaper from her front porch, I realized she was still sleeping. I didn't want to wake her up. I took the spare key from under a flowerpot at the back, let myself in through the kitchen door, made a cup of coffee, and sat on the front porch. The quiet neighborhood of Erin Woods Boulevard was waking up to another busy day. I didn't know so many people in our neighborhood went out jogging in the morning. One by one, doors opened, kids came out in school uniforms, and cars pulled out of garages and headed for the city.

"Good morning." I heard my mother's voice at the door behind me. "You came rather early today. What shift are you on?" she asked.

"Yeah, about that. I'm not going back to the hospital yet, Mom. I turned down that offer."

"No, you didn't. Tell me you didn't do anything stupid," said my mother in a shocked voice.

"No, Mom, I did nothing stupid. I think I took the most sensible decision in my life."

"What's that?" She walked back to the living room and sat on the couch. I followed her.

I told her what I had told Dr. Tyler. She didn't say another word; she left the room. Probably, Chloe would've done the same. She wouldn't have approved of this, either.

Since I had no solid plan to back me up, I didn't know how to convince my mother or anybody else that I wasn't harping on some stupid idea. I needed something concrete as fast as possible.

But the problem was I didn't know where to begin. There were thousands of genetic diseases passed on from parents to children. How could I build a protection mechanism that would shield our future generations from all hereditary genetic diseases? Well, editing the DNA of a human embryo could prevent a disease from being transmitted in a newborn, but that option wasn't available legally in most countries. Even it became available in the near future, the cost might be a deterrent. Besides, many parents wouldn't even realize they had a genetic disease until the symptoms appeared in their late thirties or early forties. By then, they had possibly already had kids. I needed the affected parents to act before they gave birth.

Dr. Tyler always used to say, "The best way to cure a disease is to understand the disease." So, without wasting much time, I concentrated on studying more on genetic diseases.

For the next few days, I went to the library in the morning and came back home in the evening and spent the rest of the night on the internet. There were more than six thousand single-gene disorders with risks of inheritance, affecting almost all parts of our body from blood, brain and nervous systems to our mental health and behavior. Lots of research was going on all over the world to cure them. Each genetic disease needed different treatments, and that kept me wondering how could I create one formula—one barricade—that would protect us from passing on the affected gene to the next generation?

But what surprised me the most was how almost every paper was talking about early detection and a possible cure in the near future—or about managing the disease well—but none said why the parents weren't getting tested before having kids. A simple genetic test before pregnancy could easily check their odds of having a baby with a genetic disorder, yet only less than twenty percent of family physicians or OB/GYN providers offered a carrier screening test in the preconception period. I wondered why the maternity and parenthood websites weren't advising any genetic tests, either. Wouldn't that awareness help reduce the number of children born with fatal genetic diseases?

Not so long ago, we had prevented deadly diseases like chickenpox, diphtheria, hepatitis B, and cholera through vaccination and immunization. We had even eradicated them from many countries. Then why couldn't we do something about genetic diseases?

I was desperate for a clue—any clue—that would help me put an end to this death sentence hanging over the children born every day with hereditary genetic diseases. In close to four months, I had been nowhere but to my room and the library. But I had achieved nothing. I was still moving in circles.

Then, one day, I received a phone call from the hospital's R&D division, "Would you like to come in for a job interview on Wednesday? We're looking for a researcher in our cardiac unit here."

"What job? Have you got the right number?" I asked the caller in disbelief. I hadn't even applied for a job there. *It must have been Dr. Tyler's doing.* Nonetheless, it sounded like a god-send to me. My savings account was fast depleting, and of late, I had been thinking a lot about Dr. Tyler's offer. Although I would've preferred to work on genetic diseases, they offered me a position in cardiac research. After all, that was my strength on paper. And two days later, after an interview, I got the job.

With a job offer in hand, I found renewed energy, and I fought back to give my idea a tangible shape before I started working the next month. I had twenty-six days left. My plan was to continue my own research in the evening even after taking the day job. After all, that was the main motivation I had when I declined the heart surgeon's position at the hospital.

But when I told my mother about the new job offer in the R&D division of our hospital, she seemed worried, but she said nothing. She knew this wasn't what I wanted; I had always aspired to be a doctor.

A few days later, one evening, I got a surprise visit from her. She walked straight into the kitchen with my favorite, pot roast chicken, in her hands. I asked, "Hi, Mom? How are you doing?"

"I brought you dinner," she said as she looked around. "I don't know how you live like this. You have takeout cartons everywhere. Your fridge has three half-eaten pizzas . . . how old are these things? I'm throwing them out, anyway. When was the last time you took out your trash? Your laundry basket is overflowing. I don't know what's going on here . . . but this isn't living."

"Sorry, Mom, give me a few more days. Did you ever come across a puzzle where you know the answer is right there in front of your eyes and you just can't seem to find it?" I tried to explain my situation.

"You know what I think? You need a break, like when you restart and reboot your computer when it freezes," replied my mother.

"I don't have time for that now, Mom."

"When was the last time you took a good look at yourself?" She dragged me to the long mirror at the other end of my room and said, "I can't even recognize you anymore. Who are you punishing, David?"

"I'm busy, Mom."

"Busy with what? Go out and live a little. Remember, we promised ourselves that?" After a short pause, she reminded me of the little pact we had made when we first got the confirmation of my HD. That day, we both had decided to live life one day at a time.

But later on, whenever I tried to make sense of that promise, it made me more confused. What life? I was breathing all right, but I was also a ticking time bomb, waiting to succumb to a deadly HD. However, when I looked at my mother's face, I knew I had to do something, at least for her sake. She had already suffered too much. "Okay, okay, I hear you, Mom. I'll go out. Maybe tomorrow."

The next morning, as I stood in front of the same mirror, I realized what had made my mother so upset. I hadn't had a haircut for quite some time. I had also stopped shaving since I went for that interview a week before. So, instead of going to the library first, I hit the hair salon.

After spending forty dollars and close to an hour, I got my clean look back. With that settled, I had only one more thing to do to get my mother off my back…but I didn't know whom I could go out with. It's not that I had no friends, but after spending every spare minute with Chloe for the last three years, they all seemed so distant. And Chloe and I were even more distant. We hadn't communicated for more than four months.

But I had almost forgotten one classmate of mine who loved to go out on a purposeless drinking night like this: Jeremy, now an orthopedic surgeon. Like always, I didn't have to explain anything. He jumped at my invitation. "I'm in. See you at Harry's at nine?" asked Jeremy on the phone.

I told him I wanted nothing too loud. He said, "Don't worry, you'll love it there."

I took his words for truth and asked, "Where is it?"

"Google it, man. There's only one Harry's on Kensington Road; you can't miss it."

After finishing my work at the library in the evening, I headed to Harry's. I had crossed Kensington Road and that part of town almost every day for the last four months, and I had seen quite a few bars and nightclubs with flickering lights. But I never knew there would be so many. Then, I saw the sign of Harry's from a distance, and I parked on the main street. I walked in, but soon a weird feeling gripped me. Was this a mistake? Should I call it off? But I also knew it would make Jeremy very unhappy. Thank god it wasn't loud inside and wasn't that crowded either. I tried to look for Jeremy, but I couldn't see him. Meanwhile, a bartender at the counter came up to me and asked, "May I get you a drink, sir?"

I grabbed a pint of beer and sat at one corner. I felt a little awkward all alone there, like a stranger in a new town. *How come Jeremy isn't here yet?* I looked at my watch; it was already five minutes past nine. The Jeremy I knew in our college days would've been there at least half an hour before time, checking out the scene. I guess now that he was a practicing surgeon, all that had changed.

Compared to my peers I was rather free. While they were busy building their careers, I was back to my student days all over again. Besides some library times and internet research at home, I had nothing else to do. Even with the R&D job, I figured little would change. But I came back to my senses as my phone beeped with an incoming message. There were also two other unread messages. Maybe I hadn't heard them while I was driving. They were all from Jeremy. The first two were about him running late and assuring me he would be here by a quarter past nine. But the third and last one made me a little sad. He wrote, "Sorry, Bro, can't make it tonight. Dr. Cline just pulled me into a major surgery. Will make it up to you."

How? I wondered. How on earth would he ever make it up to me? I didn't want to drink on another night. One was crazy enough. But the funny thing was, I didn't feel sad because he stood me up in a bar, I felt miserable because I sensed jealousy inside. I put the beer on the table and wanted to leave, but my mother's face appeared before me. I remembered what had brought me to the pub, and I didn't want to drag this thing to another night. I told myself, with or without Jeremy, I had to finish the beer there so I could be done with my night out.

I wasn't much of a drinker, but in close to twenty minutes, I had almost finished the beer. One last swig and I could be out of that place. Perhaps, the whole thing was silly, but I had never lied to my mother. *Why start now?* I picked up the glass to gulp it down, and then a girl came from nowhere. She threw an empty tray on the table and wrapped her arms around me from behind my back. "Remember me? I'm Jessie."

I was lost for a second. Then, I remembered. Sure, I knew one Jessie. No, she wasn't my friend; she was a snobbish, selfish classmate from my high school. She was also the cheerleader team captain, and it would have been a crime for her to put her arms around me in a public place like this unless she was up to something again. "Hey, Jessie!" I said while trying to see her face. *Could this evening get any worse?* But more importantly, why was she wearing an apron on top of her dress? Did she work there?

In our school days, girls like Jessie would speak with boys like me for only one reason: when they needed their homework done. After a short pause, I asked, "What do you want, Jessie? I'm sure it's not about another math problem."

"Well, I deserved that." And she touched my bicep on the right arm. "Look at you now; you filled out so nicely. See, now you have muscles."

I felt a little embarrassed, but she continued, "Wow! You know what, now you have a whole Adonis look going for you. I can't believe it. From a distance, I've been wondering who that handsome guy could be. And lucky me, it's you. What happened to those round plastic glasses?"

"Oh, I changed that to contact lenses a few years ago," I said, although I didn't know why I bothered to explain.

"See, now you look so cool. Didn't I tell you that in our school days?"

"Not exactly. Instead, you threatened to step on my glasses if I didn't change those after the spring break."

"It's the same thing, right?" And she burst out laughing. But I couldn't laugh with her. I just sat there.

Jessie realized her mistake, and she apologized. "I'm sorry. Can you please forgive me? Believe me, I'm a changed person now. Your presence kind of brought the old Jessie back in me. I suddenly remembered our school days…" Then she looked me in the eye and said, "Once again, I'm sorry."

"No apology needed, Jessie. All that had happened a long time ago," I said curtly.

"No, I gotta do this. I must apologize for my past behavior. I may have inadvertently hurt many people back then; I was stupid. You know what, I don't blame you if you hate me," said Jessie in one breath, and she looked every bit sincere.

"Hate is a very strong word, Jessie. And no, I don't hate you. It's all good now."

"Thank you…anyways, can we start over? …It's good to see you again. How are you doing?" asked Jessie as she grabbed an empty seat next to me.

"I'm good," I answered and got to my feet to leave, but one look at her awaiting face almost dragged the second part out of my mouth. "How about you?" And I knew I would regret that question.

"Can't complain. Could've been worse," Jessie replied in a solemn voice. *But how? How could Jessie's life be any worse than waiting tables in a local bar?* I would love to know. As far back as I could remember, she had ruled the school; she had both boys and girls at her fingertips. What happened? What was she doing there? I couldn't help wondering what went wrong. But she interrupted my train of thoughts. She said, "I heard you went to medical school?"

"Yes, I did. But how do you know?" It seemed she was full of surprises.

"You're kidding me? Everybody in our school knows."

I didn't know how, but I also didn't want to know. I had made a lot of efforts to make friends in my childhood days, but once I grew up and joined the pre-med, I couldn't be bothered. I concentrated on my studies, and I missed nothing.

"Tell me, who stood you up?" Jessie asked abruptly.

"Is that so obvious?" I couldn't help laughing.

"Kind of." And she laughed as well. "Since you came in, all you have done was checking your cell phone."

Once I had shaken off my hostility toward her, I actually didn't mind talking to her. But the problem was, I didn't know how to carry on. I lacked vital social skills, like chatting up girls at a bar, something Jeremy was good at. Jessie wasn't a total stranger, yet I didn't know how to continue the conversation. Not that I liked her or anything, but I didn't mind her company. I hadn't spoken to any of my classmates for a long time. But soon I was running out of subjects. What could we talk about? We had nothing in common. In a desperate attempt to continue, I asked, "How long have you been working here?"

"You want to know? Then stick around. I knock off at ten. We can go someplace quieter."

Then suddenly someone shouted, "Hey Jessie, where the fuck is our drink?" and she ran.

I looked at my watch; it was already half past nine. I was also surprised and overwhelmed. Why did Jessie want to talk to me? Anyone in that pub would've been happy to get that invitation. Why me? I was curious to find out. Even if Jessie's "prime time" was over to where she'd never be as popular as she was in her school days, she was still holding on to her short skirts and her looks. Jessie was pretty: blonde hair and blue eyes, with a born-to-be-a-cheerleader look. On top of everything, she was super-sociable, albeit with selective people. But in our school days, I had always seen her as arrogant and self-centered. Although we were in the same class, we had seldom spoken. I had been invisible to her. Then why, after so many years, she was all friendly with me?

But as I looked at her from a distance, serving drinks from one table to another, I could see she was the most popular server there. Most of the customers knew her by name. They chatted with frisky remarks; she quipped back.

"Hey, this one is on the house. Don't go anywhere." Jessie put down another beer on my table, and she vanished again. By then, the pub was teeming with customers.

Well, I had no pressing work in hand, so I didn't really mind waiting. I had also hit a brick wall in my research. I wasn't getting anywhere. After four long months, I still couldn't find any clue on how to stop the deadly genetic diseases. Maybe Dr. Tyler already knew that I was aiming for something impossible. As the days went by, I was getting frustrated. I hated my daily routine. My mother was right: I needed to live a little.

"Hi! Let's go," said Jessie, and I immediately snapped out of my thoughts. She put down her purse on the table and stood next to me.

"Do you want a drink?" I asked her.

"Nah, not here. Maybe later. Are you hungry?"

"Sure."

"Let's go to Bob's Place." And she picked up her purse.

I emptied my glass in one last swig and followed Jessie. Bob's Burger was just diagonally opposite the bar. During the daytime, that place was like a kids' playground. But at night time, it was a pub-crawler's haven; after one or two drinks, many went there for a quick bite. We found a booth at one corner and settled in. The whole thing seemed a little odd to me. I had not gone out on a date with anybody since Chloe and I broke up. Not that it was a date or anything like a date, but "Jessie and me" was truly unthinkable and, indeed, quite a mismatch. We two were from two different poles.

Face-to-face, I didn't even know what to say to her, although she didn't look all that uncomfortable. Jessie took a sip of her coffee and asked, "Now that you're a doctor, do you keep working at the hospital or do you have your own practice or something? I've no idea how that works."

Suddenly, I was in a fix. I couldn't lie to her, but the truth would open a bunch of new questions, and I wasn't in a mood to answer any of those. After all, she wasn't my friend or anything remotely close. I had bumped into her after almost ten years, and I had no plans to meet her again anytime soon. Chances were, we wouldn't even see each other for another ten years. Who knew—I might be dead by then? Although I had to admit her presence served a great purpose on my night out, and I would always remain grateful for that. She had nicely filled in for Jeremy and had saved me from lying to my mother. But that didn't mean I had to tell her everything.

My long silence had perhaps sent the wrong message to Jessie. She looked me in the eye and said, "You know what, I'm an idiot. Sure, I've no idea how to talk to you guys. Now you can laugh at me; I don't even know how a doctor's career path goes."

I interrupted her and said, "No, it's not about—"

"Let me finish first. You know what, this is the reason I avoided talking with you all my school days. I wasn't as smart as you guys. Everything I said or did always looked stupid to you. So I did the next best thing: I avoided you. And today, when I saw you again in the bar, I didn't want to run away. I thought this could be a sign, and I could get to know you. After all, we're grown-ups now."

I was flabbergasted. Who was running from whom? I didn't know Jessie had her own reasons to avoid me all this time.

I felt bad for carrying that stupid animosity for all those years. She looked sincere and genuine, and I was ready to believe what she had said earlier in the pub: she was a changed person. I told her everything about my family and my present situation. She listened with her eyes wide open, and the moment I mentioned my HD, she gasped, "Oh my god! I had no idea."

When I finally told her about my breakup with Chloe, she held my right hand from across the table and said, "I'm so sorry. You have been through so much."

Then Jessie told me how brutally her marriage had ended, just two years after her wedding. Her husband, Dylan, had walked out on them after their son, Lukas, was diagnosed with hemophilia. Jessie and her son had since moved to her mom's place, and she had been working in that pub for the last one-and-a-half years. She needed the money—a lot of money—to cope with her son's hemophilia, or simply put, bleeding disorder. It was a genetic disease that prevented the blood from clotting, often leading to uncontrollable bleeding. Factor Replacement Therapy was expensive. His hospitalizations, outpatient visits, and drug treatments often chalked up a staggering bill for her. She was spending everything she earned on her son's medical expenses.

It definitely hadn't been the life or the job she'd had in mind when she had graduated from high school. She always thought, someday, she would walk the runways as fashionistas from all over the world would watch and applaud. I felt sorry for her. I couldn't believe she had been hiding so much pain behind her smiles.

We sat there for hours re-introducing ourselves. Time passed like water falling from a high cliff. When Jessie finished her story, I couldn't help but admire her for everything she had gone through in life.

Jessie took another sip of her coffee and said, "You know what, I don't feel young anymore—I feel like I'm fifty or sixty. After a long time, when I first saw you in the bar tonight, I remembered our schooldays and it felt good: it reminded me of those carefree days."

As she lowered her head, her bangs covered the left side of her face, and I stole a quick glance. Maybe, the whole time, I got her totally wrong. With her work schedule and her responsibilities at home, she had already proven herself in life. She was organized, hardworking, and even tough. Life dealt her a hand, and she was playing to the best of her ability—without a complaint.

When we first looked at our watches, it was a quarter past three. Jessie said, "My god! I gotta go home now; I've to get Lukas ready for school by seven. We'll catch up another day."

"Sure, let's go. I'll drop you off on the way."

Jessie lived at Hillhurst, only a couple of blocks away from the pub. On normal days, she walked to work. She told me she took the job because it kept her daytime free. She wanted to be home for her son, and she also wanted to equip herself with a degree for a better future for both of them. Her mother had volunteered to look after Lukas in the evening. When I drove her back home, she thanked me and kissed me on the cheek. "I had a great time tonight after a long time. Thanks, David."

"Me too." I waved at her as she walked away, and I watched until she went in and closed the door behind her.

Chapter 5

Jessie's life story and her hardships threw me off my regular routine the next day. I went to the library on time, but I couldn't
concentrate on anything. Life had been really unfair to her.
Agreed, she hadn't been all that nice to everyone in her schooldays. But that was high school; everyone had been struggling
and fighting for their own identities. Maybe she had been a
little self-centered, but who wasn't at that age?

Still, Jessie would've survived it all, but what brought her
down was her son's sickness. And she was all alone.

Although I spent the whole day at the library, I achieved
nothing. And before I knew it, I was already at Harry's bar
again. I sat at one corner and another waiter brought me a beer.
I watched Jessie from a distance as she moved around from
one table to the next with a tray in her hand. Her face had a
unique feature, as if always smiling. Could that be the reason
why people always felt drawn to her?

But while I sat there, I felt a little embarrassed. What was I
thinking? Still, it would be even more embarrassing if I left and
she found out. I had been there less than twenty-four hours
ago, and anyone could make out that I wasn't a regular visitor
there. The rest of them kind of knew each other; they smiled,
waved, and even shared jokes once in a while. Besides, Jessie

and I had nothing in common except we both had gone to high school together. And that had happened almost ten years ago. So, what was I doing there? Was it our common misfortunes that had created a bond between the two of us? Did I feel close to her because her son and I both had life-threatening diseases? That was insane.

Jessie didn't see me until about half an hour later. She came running and hugged me. "I didn't know you were coming today."

"Neither did I," I blurted out.

"I'm so glad you're here. I've been thinking about you the whole day."

"You were?"

"Yup. I wanted to call you." She paused. "But I didn't want to scare you."

Oh my god! What the hell was I thinking? Had I just made a blunder? There was no way I could undo this. Nervously, I asked, "Did I scare you by showing up here?"

"No, silly. It means we were thinking about the same thing. Today we'll have more time because they called me in for an earlier shift. That is, if you're free."

"Sure. I'm free." I felt overjoyed as if I had won the lottery. Of late, that didn't happen very often with me. I hadn't had much luck with life in the recent months, although I didn't tell her any of that.

Still, my own reactions took me by surprise. Twenty-four hours ago, I couldn't even think of being in the same room with her, and now, her presence lit up my evening. As Jessie walked away to attend to other customers, I kept thinking, why did it feel like I had known her for ages? In our high school days, we had hardly spoken. Then, suddenly, why did I feel so close to her? And I had a feeling she felt it too. Was that a desperate attempt to cling to a partner in life? Well, I had been concentrating on my research since Chloe and I broke up, and I had not met anyone. But even if I was low on options, Jessie wasn't. I bet she could go out with anyone if she wanted to.

Maybe we both were tired and exhausted with life. Like Jessie had said the previous night, to think of it, I didn't feel young anymore, either. Dating, clubbing, or socializing all looked so meaningless.

Half an hour later, Jessie came back in a short purple dress. Responding to the surprised look on my face, Jessie explained, "We have a locker room here, and we always keep a change especially for situations like this." And she smiled.

"You look great."

Jessie smiled and flipped her hair: thick, shiny golden hair cascaded down the sides of her cheeks to fall on her shoulders. Breathtaking. She had a medium height, but she had a great figure. And naturally, she drew a lot of attention from her regular customers. But Jessie told me she wasn't looking for any of that. She thanked me for waiting and grabbed my hand. "Can we get out of here?"

Getting to know Jessie again was like meeting a stranger for the first time. Any idea I had about her in my school days proved absolutely wrong. She was outspoken but not rude; she was confident but not arrogant. Earlier I had thought she was self-centered, but I later realized that was, indeed, ambition and determination. Her personal life was an example of all that. Even in her darkest moments, she had never bowed down to pressure. She was soft from outside, but one tough fighter inside.

When we finished our dinner and got into the car, she said, "I had a great time tonight, David. I don't know how to thank you enough."

"Oh no, thank you. I had a great time too."

A while later, she looked at me and grabbed my left hand on the steering wheel. "I would love to ask you to come to my place, but you know my situation, right? I live with my mother. Besides, my son is there, and he hasn't seen me with anyone else yet."

"Of course, don't worry about it."

Jessie didn't say another word. She pulled away her hand and looked out the window. That might not have been the answer she was looking for. I felt like banging my head against the steering wheel at my stupidity. *What was that: 'Don't worry about it?'* I tried to undo my mistake. I asked, "Would you like to come to my place?"

"Sure." And she leaned on my shoulder.

When we reached my apartment, I unlocked the door and said, "Please excuse the mess."

"It looks great to me. You know what? This is exactly how I had pictured your place . . . books lying all around."

"You want a drink?"

"Water is fine. I guess the crazy drinking days are now all behind us." And she sat on the sofa.

I sat next to her, and we chatted for a while, talking mostly about me. She asked the questions, and I answered. I didn't mind; I felt connected. I hadn't had a lady in my apartment for quite some time, but it felt good. I was glad I had invited her over.

Half an hour later, when we went to bed that night, Jessie made a very interesting observation about my research. She said, "The answer to your question is in your break-up with Chloe."

At first, I didn't think she was serious, but I played along. "How so?"

She explained. "By giving up your right to become a parent, you actually stopped any chances of another child being born with HD. Isn't that what you're after?"

I sat straight up on my bed. Maybe she was on to something. Still, I wasn't sure. I nodded, and then I asked her, "But how do I convince others to do that? It's not some kind of a pill that doctors can prescribe to them."

Jessie was lying on the bed, but by then, she had also sat up and leaned back against the headboard. "It's a pill all right, but in another form. It's about spreading awareness. All you have to do is show the future parents what you have seen: the fear of ruining someone's life even before that person is born. Make the future parents aware of their own genetic diseases and the possibilities of passing them on to their children. Convince them to take a carrier screening test.

"Like you just said a while ago in the other room, most jobs require fitness tests. So why shouldn't the toughest job in the world have one? What if all grownups are made to take a fitness test before becoming a parent?"

Then her face changed color. Her eyes became cold, and her voice turned firm. "I can speak for myself: I wouldn't have had Lukas if we both got tested and we knew there were chances of putting Lukas's life in danger. I wonder why my OB never told me anything about a carrier screening test. How was I supposed to know?"

I looked at her in awe. "Holy cow! You're serious," I said, and I kissed her.

Indeed, I came quite close to that solution a few days ago, but I never thought that instead of depending on OB/GYN providers, I could spread the message myself. The solution was right there. I didn't know how she had come up with that, but I realized once again, Jessie was no average cheerleader. I had been struggling for days and months, and she had solved it in a snap. I felt grateful to her. I looked into her eyes and said, "Now, I owe you big time. I'll do anything for you."

"Anything?" and she slipped underneath the comforter with a mischievous smile on her face. She reached for the bed-side lamp with her left hand. She fumbled for a few seconds, but when she turned off the light, she whispered, "Now, prove it. No talking."

But the next morning, when I woke up, I couldn't get up. I couldn't even move. My left arm felt heavy and senseless. Jessie was still sleeping on it, and she was holding me so tight that I couldn't get myself out of the bed without waking her up. She had tucked her face in my chest, away from her pillow, and had wrapped me in her arms like a baby. I couldn't see her face, but the warmth of her body kept me glued. I felt her breathing against me. Her hair was all over my face, but I didn't mind. I was soaking in that smell, and I was thinking about what she had said the previous night.

I was so lost in my thoughts I didn't even notice when Jessie woke up. When I finally looked at her, I felt a little em-barrassed at first; she was still looking at me. I hadn't woken up with a lady in my bed in a while. I was about to get up, but she refused to leave the bed. She turned to her other side and said, "Do we have to get up now? It's so unfair. We went to sleep so late."

"Whose fault was that? Anyway, I'll go make coffee. You've got five minutes."

After coffee, I asked her to stay for breakfast. Jessie had already called her mother the previous night to ask if she could prepare her son for his preschool that morning, so she was in no hurry to get back home. I took her to my regular diner next door. The sunlight coming through the window fell on her face, and she was glowing, even with no makeup. Her golden-brown hair, though unruly, looked gorgeous. But all I could think of was how I wanted to pick her brain again. Since waking, I had been thinking about only one thing: how we could spread the word about this carrier screening test. I wanted to know how other people felt about it. I said, "Last night, you were great. Thank you."

"Thank you. You weren't bad either. In fact, you were so good you made me…"

I put down the coffee, jumped up, and I covered her mouth with my hand. I said, "You've no clue what I'm talking about, do you?" I didn't want Eliza, the diner lady, to hear about my sex life. First off, she was my mother's age, and second, she always had treated me like her son. She would be appalled. Besides, I would be too embarrassed to show my face again.

But Jessie pulled my hand away and said, "Of course, I do. I was just messing with you." And she giggled. "You should've seen your face."

However, apart from her casual banter, the breakfast turned out to be quite helpful as we discussed more about her idea. Jessie said, "First, we have to connect with people suffering from similar problems. Let's see how they feel and whether, given a choice, they would've chosen things differently. I often feel trapped, but do they? Their individual stories should create a bond, and that will give us something to build on."

We both agreed the best way forward without having much money in hand would be to spread the word through the internet. Jessie said, "Let's put up our own life experiences first. If other people also open up, then we could rally the whole world to take a decisive action."

I felt ecstatic. The dots I hadn't been able to connect during the last four months had been brought together by Jessie within the last forty-eight hours. I had been only thinking about clinical solutions, but Jessie showed me a new perspective. We could simply galvanize an existing solution that was already in place. No clinical trial, no FDA approval. I didn't know for sure where I was heading with that, but it gave me a direction. I leaned forward across the table and kissed her. "You're brilliant. Thank you."

"I like the way you say 'thank you'," said Jessie with a naughty smile.

"I can thank you all day long. Shall we head back to my place?"

"Well, I'm tempted, but I think I have to head back home now," and she smiled.

After breakfast, I drove her home and headed for the library. By then, the carrier screening thing had engulfed my mind. I couldn't wait to put it up on the internet. I used a readymade website template and created a framework. I also came up with a few suggestions for the name of the site. But I didn't want to put up anything online until I showed it to Jessie. I had realized that she would always be more of a people person. She spoke their language, and people listened to her— not because she was pretty but because she had charisma.

Chapter 6

We met at Bob's in the evening after her work. Fortunately, she had been called in early again, and she had finished her shift at eight, which gave us more time to finalize the contents of the website. I had waited all day to run everything by her before uploading anything. After all, it was her idea. Besides, I wanted to have her opinion too.

But what surprised me the most was my change of attitude toward her. After our high school, even in my wildest imagination, I had never thought our paths would ever cross in our lifetime. But ten years later, when they did—and I got to know the real Jessie behind all the makeup and attitude—she turned out to be smart, caring, and sensitive.

After brainstorming for an hour, we named the site "Parental Fitness Test." We thought it was catchy and to the point.

Jessie said, "I like it. I have a good feeling about this. Why should we exempt the world's toughest job from a fitness test? Damn it! It should be mandatory."

"Absolutely." The more I thought about it, the more passionate I felt about the idea. "You're right, parenting is the toughest job in the world, and yet it doesn't require one to prove any skill. No minimum qualification. No interviews. No selection criteria. And no genetic fitness test either. And who suffers the consequences? By the time the parents realize their mistakes, it's too late. There's no U-turn. The kids suffer silently. Whereas a simple carrier screening test could've saved the whole family from a lifelong trauma."

Jessie looked at me and added, "If the affected parents want to have kids, there're other ways too, right? How about sperm donation or egg donation? And if both partners test positive, they can always adopt."

At first, I didn't think Jessie would be so passionate about carrier screening tests. But then again, I didn't even know anything about her until three days ago. I said, "My thinking exactly."

I felt happy. After a long four months, my project had had a breakthrough. Although the idea didn't come from me, that didn't bother me. Jessie was a victim of genetic diseases too. She understood the depth and breadth of the problem, and that could be the reason why the solution had come to her so easily.

I had already written a short introduction about our website in the afternoon, but Jessie said, "It's too clinical." She put down her burger and reached for my laptop.

"Please go ahead." I pushed the laptop closer to her.

However, as Jessie pulled out her glasses from her purse, her phone rang. I had no idea she had glasses. Jessie looked at her phone screen and said, "Sorry, got to take this. It's my mother."

But soon her face turned pale as she spoke on the phone, and while talking, she shoved everything into her purse with the other hand. I asked, "What happened?"

"Gotta go. Lukas . . . bleeding nonstop . . . called 911 . . . ambulance . . . my fault . . . oh my god, it's all my fault."

From her incoherent speeches, I didn't get the full picture, but from the panic attack she was having, I gathered there was something wrong at home with Lukas.

I said, "Come on, let's go. I'm coming with you."

"Will you? Thank you. Thank you so much. My god, what have I done?"

When we reached Jessie's house, an ambulance was already there, parked in the driveway. I stopped the car on the main road in front of their house. She jumped out of the car and rushed in. I followed.

The paramedics had already put Lukas on a stretcher and were ready to leave for the hospital. I told Jessie to follow her son, and I would bring her mother to the hospital. Jessie took my hands and pressed them. She said nothing, but I could feel her hands were shaking.

The ambulance left the driveway and vanished within seconds with a screeching sound and an uncompromising loud siren, leaving behind a blurry blue-and-yellow streak of light. Her mother looked at me, confused. I said, "I'm David, Jessie's friend. We went to high school together. I can drive you to the hospital if you want."

She looked at me and said, "Thank you, dear. That'll be a great help. Let me get my coat."

On our way to the hospital, I asked, "What happened?"

"I guess Lukas was rushing down the stairs and he fell. The poor thing, he was coming to say goodnight to me. Unfortunately, when he fell, the big porcelain vase that stood at one corner of the staircase landing tumbled with him, and his right hand fell on one of the broken pieces," said Mrs. James.

"I'm sure everything will be okay." I tried to console her.

"Let's hope so, dear," said Mrs. James in a calm voice. She could be about my mother's age, in her early fifties, although she looked a bit younger with her short hair.

When we reached the Little Angels Pediatric Hospital ten minutes later, the doctors and the nurses had already taken

Lukas in. As we entered the hallway, it reminded me of my old residency days. But it didn't feel the same. This time, I was on the patients' end, worrying. If they couldn't stop the blood flow in the next hour, Lukas's life could be in real danger.

Jessie was sitting all alone in one corner of the deserted reception area like a white corpse wrapped in black. A few blood spots were still visible on her dress. While coming to the hospital, Jessie had sat by his side in the ambulance holding his bloody hand on her lap the whole time. Possibly, the blood had soaked through the bandages and had spilled over her dress. Prolonged bleeding was the worst nightmare of any hemophilia patient. Jessie looked rather pale. Her face had already assumed the worst. Her mother sat next to her, and I took the seat facing them. Jessie threw herself on her mother's shoulder. "I'm sorry, Mom. It's all my fault. I shouldn't have put the vase there."

"Jessie, dear, listen, it's nobody's fault." Her mother consoled her, but I could still hear her sobbing. I looked around awkwardly and didn't know what to do. Although I was a doctor, I couldn't offer any help. I noticed a water dispenser at one end of the corridor. I got up to get a drink for both of them.

Although the clean white walls with some pictures on both sides of the corridor was a common sight in any hospital, it reminded me of our own Hall of Fame on the final day of my interview, and I felt a little claustrophobic. As I rushed to the water cooler to get the water and get out of there, I heard voices and a loud screeching sound from behind my back. I turned around and jumped close to the wall as the paramedics wheeled in another patient. I heard someone reading out the vitals to a team of doctors and nurses on their way to the emergency room. As soon as the glass door closed behind them, the hallway was back to normal again, cold and empty with an eerie silence.

On my way back, with a cup of water in each hand, I stopped at the reception counter and introduced myself as a doctor. I wanted to get the true picture. They told me the vitals were still holding and they would get back to us as soon as they heard anything from the doctors inside.

Jessie's mother thanked me for the water. And then we waited. Jessie had leaned her head on her mother's shoulder and had closed her eyes. Maybe she was too afraid to open them again.

A while later, the girl at the reception desk came to us and said, "Good news, sir, they've stopped the blood flow. Dr. Miller will be out soon."

"Dr. Miller?" I gulped. *Is he the same Dr. Miller?* But the news had brought a new lease of life in all of us, and we immediately fixed our eyes on the big glass door in front.

Five minutes later, Dr. Miller came to Jessie and assured her that Lukas was out of danger. And it was the same Dr. Miller from my interview, but he didn't recognize me. He told Jessie, "The cut wasn't that bad. He needed five stitches. But you know how it is with hemophilia patients. There may not be a cure yet, but I assure you, it's manageable with no real danger. You need to be extra careful in his early years. You can see him now. Don't be long though: we've put him on tranquilizer for the night."

Mrs. James and I were standing next to Jessie. As she rushed to see Lukas, Dr. Miller looked at us and said, "Now you all can go back home and rest. We'll keep him through the night for observation. You can take him home tomorrow morning." He turned around and left.

However, he stopped after a few paces. He turned back, looked at me and asked, "Do I know you?"

"Not really, sir, but I met you at my board interview at Christchurch Hospital."

"That's it. I didn't know Jessie and you knew each other. Call me if you ever get tired of Christchurch. We need heart surgeons like you here. Our cardiac unit is in the next building. You should come visit us one day," he said, and he left.

Mrs. James looked at me and said, "Who are you again, son? I didn't know Jessie knew any heart surgeons."

A while later, Jessie came back. She looked happy after seeing Lukas again with her own eyes. I asked, "How's he doing?"

"He seems fine. He's sleeping though."

From the hospital to Jessie's house, it wasn't more than ten minutes' drive, but for some reason, we all went silent in the car. We were getting used to an odd reality. It's not very often you leave the youngest member of the family to spend the night alone in a hospital. When I dropped them back home, it was past midnight. Mrs. James asked, "Would you like to come in for a drink, David?"

"You guys must be tired tonight. Maybe another day."

Before Mrs. James could say anything, Jessie turned her face and said, "Please."

The living room still had blood marks on the carpet and bloody tissues scattered all over, reminding us of the life-and-death trauma of a four-year-old kid that had unfolded earlier in the evening. Mrs. James said, "Jessie, why don't you take David to your room and I'll go make tea. Do you like tea, David?"

"I would love to have tea, ma'am."

Jessie took me to her room. It wasn't impeccable, but it was nice and cozy. The room had a large bed, a writing table, a dresser, and a cupboard. Although the bed was made, the closet was wide open, and a couple of dresses were thrown all over the bed. It seemed someone had been looking for a perfect dress and had left the room in a hurry. Maybe the mess was for the black dress she was wearing. Jessie apologized, "Sorry for the mess. Sit anywhere. Maybe…you sit here." And she showed me a chair in front of her writing desk.

"After having seen my room, how can you say it's messy? It looks perfect to me." And I walked toward the chair. Jessie asked me to unzip her and then she went to change.

There were two big glass windows in the room, and one was just in front of the writing table. Through the closed window, I could see a willow tree in their courtyard and the street lights in the empty street in front. I noticed a beautiful picture of Jessie and her boy, Lukas—both smiling. Jessie looked incredible in that picture; she was glowing. I got so absorbed that I didn't even notice when Mrs. James came in with a tray in her hand. "I took that picture last year on Jessie's birthday," commented Mrs. James.

I felt a little embarrassed with the picture in my hand. I said, "It's a lovely picture, ma'am. It brings out her character."

"You're right."

Meanwhile, Jessie came back from the bathroom and asked, "What's this all about?"

I said, "Oh, we were just talking about this picture," as I put it down on the table.

"I hope it was nothing bad," remarked Jessie.

"In fact, David just said the photo brought out your character. I think it was meant to be a compliment to the photographer," said Mrs. James with a smile on her face.

Jessie fought back. "I don't think so, Mom. He must've been praising the beautiful lady in the photograph."

"Well, you can ask him," challenged Mrs. James with a smile.

Jessie looked at me. But before she could say anything, I got up from my chair and said, "I think I should go now." They both laughed.

Jessie walked me out to the gate and kissed me good night. "Thank god, everything is over, and Lukas will be back home tomorrow."

Despite Dr. Miller's assurances, I didn't sleep well that night, and I was sure neither did Jessie. *How does one sleep after coming so close to a life-and-death experience for a four-year-old boy? Life on earth isn't permanent, and there's no guarantee how long one lives, but you also don't expect your child to be constantly in danger of dying.* And all this could've been prevented with a simple carrier screening test. It made me all the more eager to know how others would react to Jessie's idea.

The next morning, I picked up a few donuts and three cups of coffee before I reached Jessie's house. She shouted to her mother as she opened the door, "Mom, David already got coffee and donuts. Let's go."

They were ready, but Jessie told me Mrs. James was doing some of her daily chores in the kitchen.

"In a minute," replied Mrs. James from the kitchen.

As I entered the house, I noticed a huge glittering sign hanging from the ceiling. It read: "We missed you last night, dude. Welcome back!"

As Mrs. James came out of the kitchen, she saw me still looking at the banner and said, "Who else but my crazy daughter? She was up until three in the morning."

"Well done, Jessie. Lukas will love it." I tried to support her hard work.

When we reached the hospital, I told them to go up and get the release papers ready, and I would be up in a minute.

Five minutes later, with a Superman costume in one hand and ten big balloons in the other, I came out of the lift on the third floor and froze. I saw Jessie sitting on a front row chair, tears rolling down her cheeks. Her mother was trying to comfort her. In a momentary lapse, I lost control of my grip and the balloons hit the ceiling. I threw the new costume for Lukas in a bin nearby and went straight to Jessie. I kneeled down in front of her seat and asked, "What happened?"

Jessie tried to say something, but I couldn't understand anything. Her lips quivered, her voice trembled, and she held me tight in her arms. She was still shivering. I looked at Mrs. James from the corner of my eyes.

"Lukas developed complications about an hour ago. They suspect it could be from last night's blood transfusion. So, they transferred him to ICU again," said Mrs. James in one breath.

From then on, we didn't speak a single word, we didn't go anywhere—we sat side by side, staring at the wall and looking at nothing and thinking or not thinking about anything. I was dreading the face of Dr. Miller again. I had no idea what would happen to Jessie if anything bad came out of his mouth. *Hadn't she suffered enough? How can I help?* Perhaps the best I could do was stay by her side, come what may. Meanwhile, I was also preparing myself for the worst.

Close to two hours and a quarter later, Dr. Miller marched out of the huge glass door in front of us with his team and headed straight to Jessie. By then, Jessie's eyes were swollen from crying. She grabbed my hand, and her grip became tighter and tighter. Dr. Miller wasn't new to loving mothers; he had been a pediatric surgeon for the last eighteen years. He said, "Don't worry. It's all good now. Shall we go to my room?"

As we reached his office, I told Jessie I could wait for them outside.

"Don't be silly," said Jessie, and she dragged me in.

Dr. Miller began. "Lukas had developed blockers to the factor. That made our blood transfusion yesterday much less effective. His platelet counts also had dropped in the morning. We didn't want to take any chances, so we put him on a specialized treatment to enable the plasma protein to help his blood clot, but don't worry, it's all good now."

Jessie got up and put her arms around Dr. Miller. Over the years, they had bonded and had developed a special relationship. Mrs. James and I also thanked him. Dr. Miller looked me in the eye and said, "Don't just thank me—be a part of us. Don't forget what I said yesterday."

As we stepped out of the room, Jessie asked, "What was that about?"

"Nothing." I tried to avoid the conversation.

But when Mrs. James told her about the job offer from Dr. Miller, Jessie responded casually, "No biggie. He has bigger plans, Ma. Just watch him."

I didn't know how to respond to that. No one had shown so much confidence in me in a while. Since I was declared HD positive and I had declined the heart surgeon's job at Christchurch Hospital, everyone had thought I was on a downward spiral. Jessie's words gave me new hope. After a long time, I felt good about myself again.

Chapter 7

Three days later, we brought Lukas back home. I dove into our project again, and Jessie went back to work. Jessie's words in the hospital were still ringing in my ears: "He has bigger plans, Ma." *But is she harboring more confidence in me than I have in myself?* I knew we had undertaken a mammoth task. Success wasn't totally in our hands. It depended on how the rest of the world would view it. But more than anything, Lukas's accident reminded me of the uncertainty of my life, too. I had to make carrier screening tests for parental fitness a reality everywhere before the onset of my HD.

I looked at our website proposal again and wanted to go live without further delay. I called Jessie in the afternoon. "We've got to get the website ready as early as possible. We have to get the word out."

We met in the evening after her work. In the last few days, Bob's had become our regular meeting place. I told her I would re-write the intro. "You can look at it tomorrow. But what I want you to do is write your story. How Lukas has changed your life—the good, the bad, and the guilty feeling."

"I don't know about that, David. Are you sure?" Jessie tried to avoid going public with her situation. She didn't want anyone to feel sorry for her.

But I tried to convince her with her own words. "Like you said, parents blame themselves after a kid is born with an inherited genetic disease. Your experience can help them understand that even if the disease doesn't affect them, it can still change their kids' lives the way it did with you and Lukas."

Jessie's eyes welled up and tears came to the brim, but she was trying her best to hold everything back: her tears, her anger, and her emotions. By the time I realized the pain I had caused, it was already too late. She ran to the bathroom. I wanted to apologize. *What the hell was I thinking? How could I be so insensitive?*

Five minutes later, Jessie came back to our booth. I had already ordered a hot chocolate for her. That was her comfort drink—much like other's comfort food—as I had found out in the last few days. I said, "I'm sorry, Jessie, I don't know what came on to me. I spoke without thinking. Since we brought Lukas back home, I could think of only one thing: we're running out of time. But I was being selfish, and I'm sorry."

"You've nothing to be sorry about, David. I know you're doing this for the greater good. I understand that, but you know what they say: 'truth stings.' Don't worry; I'll be okay." She smiled from the corner of her eyes and took a sip of the hot chocolate. "Let's do it."

A moment later, she added, "But before we go online, maybe we should send the draft to my sister, Lucy. I'll talk to her tonight. After all, she has been doing this for the last four years."

"I didn't know you had a sister. But any help will be great."

"Well, now you know. But she doesn't live here; she's in Chicago, working in a software company," explained Jessie.

The next day, we changed our meeting place to Jessie's house. That way, she could stay closer to Lukas. After what had happened, she wanted to be extra vigilant during his growing years. When Jessie told her mother about our new mission, she extended her full support for everything. "Just tell me what you guys need. I'm all yours," said Mrs. James.

"Can you start with coffee, Mom?" Jessie quipped.

"Yes, boss. Three coffees coming up," she replied with a smile, and we all laughed like in any normal family. But deep in our hearts, we all knew neither Jessie's nor mine would ever be a normal household. We would have bad days and good days, but more painful days would probably run our lives. That's why our laughter was so special and our cheerful moments felt so dear to us.

As we settled in, Jessie showed me her write-up. I read the whole piece in one breath. It was intimate, emotional, and engaging. I felt dazed. I heard Jessie's faint voice as if from a distance—she mentioned something about my coffee. I came back to my senses as soon as I felt the warm coffee mug on my right hand.

"Oh yeah. Thanks."

I looked at the screen again and said, "I didn't know you could write so well."

"You don't know a lot of things about me, mister."

"Like what?"

"Close the door and I'll show you."

"Are you crazy? Your mom is here."

"So? She'll come and say, 'Jessie, you're grounded,' right?" She giggled, and her hair fell over her face.

I couldn't stop laughing at the way she had spoken, mimicking her mother's voice. After a while I said, "Now that your mother is part of our team, maybe we should all go out for dinner and celebrate the launch of the website. What do you say? You should bring Lukas too. How about this Saturday?"

Jessie looked at me and said, "I love that idea. It definitely calls for a celebration." She bent toward me and kissed me.

I felt a little embarrassed as I heard Mrs. James's voice at my back. "Am I interrupting something?"

"Not at all." I jumped to my feet from the chair like a teenage boy.

After hearing about our dinner plan from Jessie, Mrs. James looked at me and said, "Well, it's my treat then."

"But it's supposed to be our celebratory dinner for the website, ma'am."

"So what? Now, I'm a part of this project too. It's my treat, and Saturday it is." And she left.

That Saturday, I had a great time at dinner with Jessie and her family. We went to Lukas's favorite—Ming's Palace—a local Chinese restaurant, and it turned into a double celebration: our website launch and Lukas's get-well party. Lukas was a fine kid, but a four-year-old boy could be also quite a handful. I didn't even know how to answer some of his questions. But Jessie and her mother knew what to do. They never grew tired of his inquisitive mind; they loved to answer them all. But sometimes they simply asked, 'What do you think, Lukas?' and let him figure out his own answers in his little four-year-old way of looking at the universe.

Later in the evening, when Jessie went upstairs to tuck Lukas in, Mrs. James told me how Jessie had celebrated every milestone Lukas had crossed. She clapped non-stop when he first started kicking, throwing and catching a ball. She picked up Lukas on her shoulder and ran around the house the day he walked down the stairs. She cried out in joy the first time Lukas picked up one of her photos from the dresser and said, "Mommy." She always had time for his questions—she would make time. Nothing was more important to her than him.

The next day, my telephone rang very early in the morning. I didn't want to get up yet on a Sunday, but I feared it could be from Jessie. And for obvious reasons, I assumed the worst. I didn't even look at the screen as, nervously, I answered, "Hello?"

"Did I wake you up?" asked my mother.

Although I felt relieved, my mother's voice immediately engulfed me with terrible guilty feelings. I said, "Don't worry about it, Mom. Sorry I didn't call you the last couple of days. Anyway, what's up?"

"How are you? What have you been doing? Aren't you supposed to start work tomorrow?"

"I start work on the following Monday, Mom, not this one. How are you doing?"

"I'm good. You better go back to sleep."

"I can't sleep now."

"Then why don't you come for breakfast? I'll make dosa." And with that, my mom threw in the ultimate bait. Dosa is a form of Indian pancake, popular in the southern part of India. I always had loved that taste, but no restaurant in Calgary had dosa on their menu.

"I'm on my way." I hadn't had dosa for quite some time. I also hadn't had time to talk to her for the last few days—I had been super-busy with Lukas's accident and all that. At breakfast, I told my mom everything about Jessie and about our new website launch. After I finished, she asked, "You like her, huh?"

"It's funny you only got that from everything I said."

"When you can't finish a sentence without having her name in it, that person must mean a lot to you." My mother smiled.

"I don't know, Mom. She's just an old friend."

"Are you sure about that?"

"Well, no, Mom. I don't know. Maybe more…but I'm not sure. Anyway, I should go now…I want to hit the supermarket before it gets crowded."

My mother had caught me totally off-guard. I wasn't ready to answer any of those questions. I hadn't figured out anything yet. *Do I want another relationship?* Wouldn't that lead to the same ending? That wouldn't be fair to Chloe. *But why not?* Jessie already had said she wouldn't want to have more kids. But the situation was totally different with Chloe, and it wouldn't have been fair to deprive her of something that was so important to her. I still thought we had done the right thing. In fact, as a victim of a genetic disease, Jessie understood my situation better. *Still, isn't it too early to think about all that even before we started dating?* I blamed my mother for putting all that in my head in the early morning. *Who knows what Jessie wants?* Maybe I was just an old high school friend to her—but somehow, I doubted that.

A sudden phone call from Jessie brought me back to reality. I had already walked into my neighborhood supermarket, part of my routine weekly chores, and was standing in front of the meat counter when I answered, "Hey! What's up?" I pushed the trolley to one corner to avoid stalling others.

"You better sit down," said Jessie.

"What happened?"

"Guess what? Our site got two hundred and thirty-one hits in a day, and thirteen comments from parents, one from a patient, and one from a teacher."

"Wow! I can't wait to see this," I replied.

"Where the hell are you?" She sounded impatient.

"I'm at the supermarket."

"Screw the supermarket. This is bigger than what we expected, right?"

"Much bigger. I'm on my way." I pushed aside the cart and left the supermarket.

I didn't have a clue what Jessie's sister had done to that site after we had sent her the rough draft. I hadn't met her yet, but Jessie had only good things to say about her. Jessie had said, "Don't worry, Lucy is nothing like me. Sometimes I wonder whether we are real sisters. She's the nerdy type."

After Jessie had told her about our project, she wanted to help us too. Two days ago, Jessie had informed me that Lucy would re-design the site for clarity and would also optimize the website for search engine use. She had also linked our site to many other blog posts. I didn't know what she meant by all that, but it had worked. In our first day, we'd already gotten way more hits than expected.

However, as soon as I entered her room, Jessie gave me a kiss. I asked, "What's that for?"

"I'm just happy," claimed Jessie.

New comments were pouring in every ten to fifteen minutes, and they were from all over the world. It was like the live telecast of a reality show.

Cindy Sheldon wrote from Austin, Texas, about her pretty little daughter suffering from sickle-cell disease. Megan Maurice from Edmonton talked about her ten-year-old son, Brandon, fighting hemochromatosis— also known as iron overload. Jason Dubey wrote from Nigeria about the uphill battle his mother was facing every day with dementia.

I didn't even notice when Lukas came in with a ball in his hand and stood by my side. He nudged me with one hand and asked, "You want to play?" Before I could say anything, Jessie jumped in. "Okay, okay. Let's go, Lukas."

"Not you, Mom, I want to play with David," said Lukas.

I said, "Come, let's go." I turned to Jessie and told her to continue reading. I would be back soon.

But I had sure underestimated a young boy's energy level. We played for almost an hour, and in spite of running and chasing, there wasn't a shred of tiredness or any sign of reprieve until Mrs. James rescued me. She said, "It's lunchtime, Lukas."

When we finally stopped reading those comments later that day, it was seven-thirty in the evening. Mrs. James said out loud, "Jessie, I'm not serving dinner in your room . . . you guys gotta come here and eat."

I had to admit, she had done enough in a day. We had been stuck to our computers from the minute I went in, and I had heard Jessie had been like that all morning. Mrs. James had taken care of Lukas the whole day, served us lunch, and even made coffee for us.

I said, "Let's call it a day," and I quickly went down to apologize to Mrs. James.

After dinner, I wanted to head back home. But as we sat down on the front porch and talked about all those comments and posts again, we lost track of time. I told Jessie to convey my appreciation to her sister. "Thank her on my behalf. She must've spent a lot of time changing the site. I must admit, she has made it more user-friendly."

Lucy had divided the website's comment section into four categories: from parents, patients, siblings, and others, which included friends and relatives. Each group had their own private space. Those willing to tell their stories could do so with one click. However, the most vital section was the readers' opinions on introducing a Parental Fitness Test for all. The header read: "Every Vote Counts: please sign up for a carrier screening test today." And the overall result was amazing.

But that part also brought in most of the condemnations. Some criticized us for meddling with the natural procreation process and for being insensitive to peoples' wishes to having kids. A couple of comments were particularly ruthless. I told Jessie, "We have to tread carefully. Of course, not everyone will be on board with genetic testing. Otherwise, carrier screening tests would've taken off a big way a long time ago. By rights, it should've been just like all the other regular tests for pregnant parents."

I took Jessie's hand and continued. "But forget those nay-sayers. Did you notice there are two things common in most responses?"

"What's that?"

"People are almost unanimous in recognizing the power of parental fitness tests…and they all applauded your struggle in life with Lukas's hemophilia."

Jessie smiled, but it wasn't a happy smile. It appeared at the corner of her lips and faded as quickly as it had come. The vivid description of how her world had changed within the first three months after she had given birth to Lukas could make anyone cry. She had been back to the hospital with Lukas on the eighty-third day. As the doctors took her baby to the ICU, she and her then-husband, Dylan, sat there waiting for more bad news to follow.

She had recounted those steps in her story in a candid manner. "The doctors had diagnosed Lukas with hemophilia A, a condition where patients suffer from the lack of a plasma protein, medically known as blood clotting factor VIII. That day, I didn't understand what all those words meant. Every time I looked at Lukas's face, I didn't know whether I should feel angry or be sad for him. But the moment he smiled, I knew there would be glimpses of happiness too."

Her story wasn't about herself. She had only one line about her husband. She wrote, "He preferred to leave the battlefield, and I said okay." She wrote how fear and anxiety had filled her world at first. She was worried sick when Lukas went to play-school—she waited in her car outside for four hours, worrying about him falling and bleeding to death. What if another kid accidentally hit him or pushed him down the stairs? A few months later, once she had begun to wait for him at home, she would jump every time the phone rang. Her worst nightmare was a call from the school nurse. What if she couldn't reach there in time? Although she had provided all the emergency contacts and the dos and don'ts with profuse bleeding, she still couldn't rest. She had also given Lukas's hematologist's contact number to the school administration office. But all those pre-cautions didn't stop her from worrying about the most uncer-tain "what-ifs." While other mothers had to worry about their kids fitting in, making friends, and getting bad grades, she knew those might never cross her mind. That would have been a luxury to her. She had no idea how to get past her paranoia and feel like a normal mother again.

Similar stories emerged from all over the world. People had hoped for a fairytale life before they were hit by the hard truth of reality, but they all felt the same way about the pa-rental fitness test. Many confessed they had no idea that there was an iota of chances of passing on a deadly disease to their children. OBs had told them to dig into their family's medical history, but they were never offered a carrier screening test. *Why?*

While family history provided helpful information, my research showed that a whopping eighty percent of children born with recessive diseases had no known family history. Only a carrier screening test could've detected that.

They were sad, but they all agreed they would've loved to go through a carrier screening test before bringing someone into this world with any major complications. Alice from

Copenhagen wrote, "Life, as it is, is uncertain. Why add more odds to it?"

Suddenly, Mrs. James opened the front door and said, "Well, good night, David. Good night, Jessie; I'm turning in."

I looked at my watch and got a shock; it was a quarter past midnight. "I gotta go too. Later, Jessie. Good night, Mrs. James," I said, and I rushed out.

When I reached home, I couldn't resist the temptation to take another look at the numbers. I opened my laptop. The total comments had reached five hundred and sixty, and the number of hits stood at fourteen thousand plus. I texted the latest numbers to Jessie and went to bed.

"I know," she texted back.

I didn't think I could sleep that night. Before publishing the site a few days ago, I had thought, definitely, some people would share their stories, but I had never expected that kind of response. Never had I thought we could reach out to thousands of people without going anywhere and without talking to anybody in person. All my life, I had heard about the power of the internet, but this was the first time I had experienced it myself. After some pretty rough things in my life, I saw a ray of hope. I remembered what Dr. Tyler had said on our first day in medical school: "You'll learn a great deal about medicine and surgery here and how to cure and manage many life-threatening diseases, but you must never forget that preventing a disease is always better than a cure."

I also learned something new that day from those comments: how adversities had made those parents strong. They never gave up; they rather took everything as a challenge. Where did all that strength come from? Ordinary happy-go-lucky men and women in their twenties suddenly turned into super-parents. They gave up everything that their disease-stricken child couldn't do—no regrets. For some families, they hadn't gone on a vacation for ages. Some didn't go to movies or to a ball game because they couldn't take their kids, and instead, they watched it at home, with their kids. And the best thing was, none of them had any regrets for not being able to do any of that. Josephine from Ireland said, "I don't have time even to catch up with my old friends for a cup of coffee, but you know what, I have a new friend now—my daughter, Emily."

But they all had one thing in common: they regretted the fact that they were the cause of their children's sufferings.

I remembered what Joey wrote from Auckland, "I never knew I could survive so many sleepless nights. I needed my full eight hours of sleep even during my exam time. Otherwise, I would be totally dysfunctional the next day. But now I don't even remember when was the last time I had a good night sleep. My son, three-year-old Jimmy, was diagnosed with cystic fibrosis last month. I know, someday, I will sleep again, but not now. After my office and my house chores, whenever I have time these days, I look at his face, even while he is sleeping. And that makes me happy."

I looked at my watch; it was close to two in the morning. But surprisingly, I wasn't feeling sleepy at all. I felt fresh, as though I could go for a run. However, thinking about the up-hill task we had against the various opposing groups—and the hundreds of 'thank you' replies due the next day—I turned off the light and went to bed. I felt happy with the progress, but I was sure none of these would've happened without Jessie. If I hadn't met her in the bar that night, I would be still moving in circles. My R&D job that had seemed so precious a few days ago didn't look that attractive anymore. With Jessie's help, I had finally found a way forward. *Now, I have to make the Parental Fitness Test Program a reality before the onset of my disease.*

Chapter 8

My mother used to say, "Don't look at the distance. Put your one foot in front of the other, and soon you will reach your destination." Anytime I felt overwhelmed with a new thick book, that advice had helped. I was planning to follow that guidance again. The response to our website in support of the parental fitness test exceeded my expectations. Many recommendations and suggestions came pouring in. The huge support also brought new responsibilities. And it was time to act. I called Jessie as soon as I finished my morning coffee.

"Hey! Good morning," Jessie greeted.

"Did you see what Alex Tanner wrote last night?" I asked.

"At what time did he post it? There are so many comments. Tell me the time, so I can jump to that."

That was true. Comments kept coming. So I read it out to her. Alex wrote, "Don't you think like sex education, the basics of hereditary genetic disorders must be taught in schools before the boys and girls become sexually active? The young generation should know that the consequences could be more than a pregnancy. Sometimes, without knowing whether they're carrying any hereditary genetic disorders in their genes, it can result in giving birth to a child with a severe genetic disease."

Jessie said, "I agree with Alex."

"Yes, me too." Then I told her about my mother's advice. "So, one step at a time. Let's get to the parents and soon-to-be parents first, and later maybe we can see how to spread the awareness through sex education at the school level."

"Hey, how about this one?" Then she read out what Mika wrote from Berlin: "Like conscientious partners always take voluntary tests of HIV and other STDs before having sex, aspiring parents should also test themselves to rule out the possibilities of carrying any hereditary genetic disorder."

"Absolutely. See . . . people are opening up," then I paused as I was trying to read an email from my new office about the present status of a research—I would be taking over on Monday. Naturally, they wanted me to be in the loop. But realizing I still had Jessie on the line, I quickly added, "I think we have a real shot at this."

"Then why your voice says something else? You sound distracted. Is there anything you aren't telling me?" asked Jessie.

The email from the office caught me by surprise and reminded me again about my joining date the next week. I said, "You realize that these people will now look to us for answers. We must organize ourselves fast; in fact, just reading all the comments in one day by a single person already seems impossible. And I have to start work next week. They just sent me an email, and I was trying to read that—I'm sorry. But what can we do?"

"We'll do the best we can. Don't worry, we'll manage. Besides, you'll be there to help in the evening, right? My mom can help out too. And I'm sure we'll get some volunteers soon."

However, I had to end our conversation abruptly as an important reminder popped up on my phone. On top of everything, that morning, I also had my appointment with Dr. Bergmann. I would've loved to skip it, but I had already missed the last two and that had made Dr. Tyler very unhappy. He had said, "You should know better. Hospital protocols are there for reasons. You may be one goddamn exception, but why take chances?"

If not for anything else, I had to go for Dr. Tyler's sake. Besides, I also owed him a visit. I hadn't updated him for a long time, and he would be so happy to hear about this break-through.

I had a great session with Dr. Bergmann that day. I told her all about our Parental Fitness Test Program, and she encouraged me to give my best efforts, irrespective of the results. After the session, I headed to see Dr. Tyler. But my heart sank as soon as I entered his room. I saw Chloe waiting while Dr. Tyler was rummaging through heaps of papers dumped on the round table in his room. For a few seconds, I froze. But Dr. Tyler looked at me and said, "What a coincidence! I was just talking about you in their class today. Remember, David, you wrote a piece for our quarterly research journal on 'How to take care of your heart without medication?' It was published sometime around this time last year. I want them to read it, but I can't seem to find it here, and I have to go. I'm afraid I might be late for my meeting. Do you have a copy, David?"

"I might have. I'd have to look for it, sir."

"Well, it's settled then. You pass her a copy once you find it." He looked at Chloe and then looked at me again and said, "By the way, this is Chloe. Chloe, this is David."

I wanted to tell him that I already knew her, but before I could open my mouth, he said, "Now, go, go, go. I've already wasted a lot of time looking for the damn paper," and he called out for his secretary, Alice.

As I was getting out of his room, he asked, "David, did you see Dr. Bergmann?"

"Yes, I did, sir. Everything is fine. I'll come back another day."

"Please do that."

Chloe and I got out of his room and walked a few paces with an awkward silence. Then, Chloe asked, "How are you doing? And why are you seeing Dr. Bergmann?"

There was no point in hiding the truth from Chloe anymore. She knew who Dr. Bergmann was. I said, "I'm HD positive, Chloe. But I'm good…and you?"

Chloe didn't answer me. She asked, "How come you never told me?"

"I didn't think this was something worth announcing. And I'm really fine until the onset of the disease." To ease the situation, I asked her again, "Tell me how you're doing."

"I am good too. Just too much pressure…but you wouldn't know much about that, though, because you were always a good student."

"You're quite good too. By the way, do you really want that article?"

"Yeah, of course? Dr. Tyler wants me to make copies and distribute them to the rest of the students in my class."

"In that case, why don't I email you a soft copy? That will be easier to share."

"Thanks, David. But if you aren't rushing for anything, I would love to have a coffee with you." She paused, looked at her watch and continued. "I have about half an hour before the next class starts."

"Sure, I would love to have coffee," I answered as I also wanted to talk to her. To think of it, the last time we'd seen each other, we had left everything abruptly.

We walked to the cafeteria, picked up our coffee, and sat down at one corner. Chloe asked, "But why didn't you tell me you were HD positive?"

"Does it matter?"

"Yes, it does. Now people might think I'm a horrible person."

"Why would they think that?"

"Because I broke up with an HD victim."

"Remember, you didn't know it at that time."

"The truth is, I guessed as much, and I panicked. I'm sorry, David."

"What are you sorry about? That was only a natural reaction. We were all overwhelmed with the uncertainties at that time. Don't beat yourself up."

"But I truly loved you."

"I know. Tell you what, we can always stay friends if you want to."

"I'd like that very much." She paused and asked in a genuinely concerned tone, "What are you doing these days?"

"Oh, nothing much, although I will be joining the cardiac R&D here next week."

"Really? That's great news. Then chances are, I'll see you more often." She paused as she took a sip of her coffee. "Are you dating anyone?"

Was I? It took me a minute to answer. Seeing Jessie every day for our project and casual sex wouldn't technically count. We hadn't even gone out on a date yet, and on top of everything, I didn't even know how Jessie felt about me. So, I said, "No, not really, but I'm close."

"Who is she?" asked Chloe.

"I'll tell you another day. And you?" I tried to divert the conversation.

"No," she said curtly. Then, Chloe turned her head to the left and drew my attention to an empty table at the other corner. "Remember that table? That's where we first met."

"Of course, I remember . . . every bit of it. How could I forget?"

I had first met Chloe in the same cafeteria about three years before when I had just started my residency and Chloe was in her sophomore year in our medical school. She was also my classmate Megan's cousin.

That day, when we all had entered the cafeteria after our usual round, we found two girls occupying our regular big table at the east wing corner. We looked at each other—we could've sat at any other table, but there was always a comfort level associated with sitting at the same table, like sleeping on the same side of the bed.

Megan said, "Don't worry, she's my cousin. I'll ask them to move to another table. I wonder why they're here."

I said, "I heard the school cafeteria is closed for one week for renovation."

However, Jeremy had a different idea. He proposed, "Or, they could join us."

"No way," Megan had objected. "They're too young. Besides, she's my cousin."

But Megan couldn't do much to protect her cousin that day. Jeremy took the lead after Megan introduced us to Chloe and her friend, Joanne—a cute-looking Chinese girl. Jeremy had a thing for the oriental looks, although I was sure he couldn't make out any difference between the Chinese, Japanese, or the Koreans. After they had finished their lunch, as Chloe and Joanne were leaving, Jeremy surprised us all. "So, it's a double date then," and he looked at me. "Chloe and you . . . Joanne and I."

I asked, "What date?"

Megan said, "What are you talking about?"

"We aren't going out on a date with you guys," protested Joanne.

But Jeremy insisted. "We'll pick you up at seven on Friday."

"Good luck with that. We aren't giving you our addresses. Pick us up if you can find us," said Joanne, and they walked away.

"You don't have to give us your address. You're a student here, right?" Jeremy shouted from behind their backs.

That was our first meeting. I hadn't had an opportunity to speak with Chloe, and she had also said little. Still, I thought I would have loved it if, by any chance, Jeremy's wild dream came true. And believe it or not, Jeremy found Joanne's hostel, and the rest was easy. I never knew how Jeremy pulled it off, but we all went out on that date.

Three years later, much had changed. Jeremy and Joanne had dated for close to four months, but it soon fizzled out. I looked at Chloe and asked, "Do you remember Jeremy?"

"Oh my god! That guy was crazy." Then, she looked me in the eyes and asked, "Never mind Jeremy, what did you do the last few months?"

At first, I didn't want to tell her anything about the parental fitness test thing. I already knew her point of view, so I didn't want to rub it in. But Chloe insisted. "Don't tell me you were sitting idle at home for the last four months. That's not you. I wouldn't buy that."

I told her briefly about what Jessie and I had been doing. "The response so far is good, and we want to pursue this further. But we need volunteers; we can't even cope with all the email replies. And soon we have to start visiting OB/GYN providers too. I'm not sure how we can take it forward. On top of that, I'll join here full-time next week, and I won't be able to give much time."

After hearing everything, Chloe asked, "Who is this Jessie? Is she a doctor too?"

"No, she isn't. But she feels strongly about the issue."

"Oh, I see." I didn't know what Chloe thought for a minute, but she said, "Don't worry, I can help you guys for three hours from Mondays through Fridays with your admin work."

"Are you sure?" I asked. Although that would be very helpful, I wasn't sure whether it was a good idea.

Then she said, "But I want something in return. I want you to tutor me if I need any help."

"Well, I think I can do that. But I need to discuss this with Jessie. I will let you know."

We parted with a hug. It was our first meeting after the breakup. We both needed a closure, and the accidental meeting certainly helped us in getting one. We both had established we were moving on. Still, I wasn't sure whether Chloe coming to help would be a good idea, so I mentioned nothing to Jessie. But circumstances forced me to change my mind two days later when Jessie almost broke down one afternoon.

"I told you 'no,' Lukas. A 'no' is a 'no'. Which part of it don't you understand?" I heard Jessie screaming from upstairs. That might sound like a common line in any ordinary house-hold, but Jessie's wasn't an ordinary one. She had never raised her voice at Lukas. She always reasoned with him, however illogical it might have sounded to others. Most likely, it was more about Jessie than it was about Lukas. I got out of the living room and looked for Mrs. James to find out what had ignited all that commotion.

"What's going on upstairs?" I asked when I caught up with her in the kitchen. Mrs. James was preparing the afternoon tea.

"She's been this way for the last few days. Maybe she isn't sleeping enough. And how can you sleep enough when you go to bed after three or four in the morning?" complained Mrs. James while arranging the tray. "But hey, don't take it out on the poor boy."

"But what's she doing up so late?" I blurted out.

"She says she has to answer all the emails until any volunteer comes in."

What a colossal pressure that must have been. And it was all my fault. I dragged her into this. I said, "Don't worry, Mrs. James, I'll get it all sorted out today. And thank you for telling me this."

As I walked back to the living room, I stopped at the staircase for a while. *Should I tell her about Chloe's offer to volunteer right now? . . . Maybe I should give her some time to cool off first.*

Before Jessie went out for her evening shift at the bar, I told her what Chloe had offered. Jessie asked, "Chloe? You mean your Chloe?"

Did I hear a voice of disapproval? "Yes, that's why I didn't even mention it," I quickly emphasized.

"But why? We need help, so why not?" asked Jessie.

I had no straight answer to that question. We were swamped, and we needed more manpower to cope with all the work. Although we had received several offers to help, they were from cities in other countries and none from Calgary. Many had already started helping their local teams. We wanted to build a core group in each country, and let them take the lead in their respective areas. Local groups would always have a better understanding of their culture and laws. But we also needed people to help us grow in Canada. So I told her everything about my accidental meeting with Chloe and asked, "What do you think?"

"I think it's a great idea. But why didn't you tell me?" she asked. "Unless you didn't want her here."

"No, I don't care. But you know how she thinks about the whole thing, right? She still wants to take the risk of having kids despite knowing she or her partner might carry a deadly genetic disease. She believes in chances. And we don't."

"Do you think a mason building a church believes in God as strongly as the priest does? Damn it, she offered to help and you're still hesitating? Besides, one day, she might change her stance."

I didn't know what to say. Jessie had a solid argument, so I kept quiet. She added, "We really need more people to grow locally. How can we ever organize workshops here with no help? Neither of us can stop working and go full-time on this because we need our salaries. I tell you what, if it doesn't work out, you can always let her go."

We both agreed that there was no need for any formal interview. Jessie spoke with her on the phone, and she seemed pleased. Chloe told her she would join us two days later, on the next Monday.

Over the weekend, Jessie and I worked very hard to give our workplace a professional look. Mrs. James gave us her study, and we tried our best to make it look like a small office. Since Jessie's father had passed away, the room hadn't been used much. There were heaps of carton boxes full of old clothes, books, toys, and god knows what. "I don't know why we keep this stuff," said Jessie.

"Sentimental values?" I asked softly.

"I have no idea. Anyway, we can dump them now in Lucy's room, but she'll be coming back next weekend when she attends a meeting in Toronto. We gotta clear it by then. Otherwise, she'll kill you."

"Why me? You're her sister," I quipped.

"Okay, okay, she'll kill us both." Jessie laughed.

On Monday evening, as Jessie and I were working in our new office, Chloe stepped in. Jessie dropped everything and ran to welcome her, "Hi! I'm Jessie . . . we spoke on the phone."

"Chloe Clayton," she introduced herself, and they shook hands. Then Jessie briefed her about the work.

After a while, Chloe looked at me and said, "Hey! How are you doing?"

"I am good. And you?"

"I'm good too. And oh, thank you for calling, though." Then she lowered her voice and whispered, "But I have to admit she's pretty. Are you two…"

I felt embarrassed and quickly got up from my seat. "What are you talking about?" Chloe's remarks were so uncalled for. I turned around to look at Jessie's face.

"Don't worry, she isn't here," assured Chloe.

"Still, you shouldn't say such a thing."

"Okay, okay, you're the boss," she said, and she looked at her computer screen.

I had no idea when Jessie had slipped out of the room. Precisely, for this reason, I hadn't wanted Chloe there. It would probably be a colossal waste of time with this kind of nonsense.

"Will you please excuse me for a minute?" And I went out of the room, looking for Jessie.

I found her in the kitchen, making tea for our new volunteer. I asked, "Are you mad or what?"

"Why? What happened?"

"Why did you leave?"

"I came here to make tea for our guest."

"She isn't a guest in your house, she's volunteering."

Jessie ignored what I had said. "Come, let's get to work. We have a new volunteer."

Thank god, Chloe didn't say anything embarrassing the rest of the evening. Maybe Jessie was right: it was nothing, and I was just over-thinking.

Before leaving for the day, Chloe came up to my table and said, "Well, I gotta go. I finished everything and left a note on Jessie's desk."

"Thanks, Chloe, for doing this."

"Glad I could help. Good night." And she left.

Chloe's coming to volunteer for us didn't turn out as dreadful as I had imagined, although there were occasional comments from Chloe that were uncalled for. One afternoon as Jessie brought coffee for Chloe and tea for me, Chloe asked, "Since when do you drink tea, David?" The truth was we had been together for three years, so she was more familiar with my choices and she knew I loved coffee and didn't fancy tea.

But what she didn't know was that since I had met Jessie and her mother, I had taken a liking to tea as well. First, I looked at her, then at Jessie. They both were waiting for my answer. I didn't want to hurt either of them, so I said, "While I was growing up, my mother never had time. She was always rushing and had used only teabags at home, but now I have learned that it takes more than just hot water and teabags to make good tea. It really tastes different here; you should try it sometime."

However, I also didn't want to escape the truth. I told Jessie the next day about my preference for coffee. She had one question: "Why didn't you tell me? I hate to hear from others."

I knew what she meant. I assured her it would never happen again.

The situation with Chloe in the same office wasn't ideal, but we needed help. And Chloe was a good worker. She was smart and sincere. As days went by, more and more heart-aching stories poured in. People from all over the world applauded our efforts. Other websites for genetic diseases also thanked us for spreading the awareness and had linked our site to their own. However, with appreciation came a host of criticisms. Many said, "Children are God's gifts, and you have no right to meddle with that."

We didn't want to get into any arguments. We explained ourselves as clearly as we could. We told them we had no intention to meddle with the wishes of anyone, let alone the all-mighty God. We were simply trying to protect our future generations from some deadly diseases. It was a fight against human sufferings, but the ultimate decision rested with each individual.

We also received flak from parents whose children were suffering from chromosome abnormalities. Mrs. Blatter wrote, "What about my son? He's suffering from Down syndrome. How could I have stopped that with carrier screening tests?"

I had no answer to that. And like most people, in the beginning, Jessie also didn't know the differences between the single-gene diseases and those that came from chromosome abnormalities. To make things simple, I gave her a list of all single-gene diseases that could be passed on from parents. And Jessie put the rest in a separate folder for me to answer later, and those letters were piling up. But when Chloe saw Mrs. Blatter's email, she said, "For heaven's sake, you're a doctor; you can't sit on a letter like that. It's a desperate attempt for a mother to reach out."

"I know, but what can I say? I have no solution to offer."

Jessie said, "Don't bother, we already have our hands full."

"We'll always have our hands full," rebutted Chloe. Then she looked at me and said, "We have to let her know that Down syndrome is a chromosomal condition and ours is an effort to stop single-gene diseases. By familiarizing people with carrier screening tests, we expect parents to stop passing on deadly diseases unknowingly to their children. We feel for her and for her son, but her son has an extra copy of chromosome 21. Scientists and doctors are pursuing cures for Down syndrome and other chromosome abnormalities, and we look forward to the day when such things can be avoided."

"Then why don't you write it?" I asked Chloe.

"Because I'm not a doctor yet. I think it should come from you."

I looked at Jessie. She wasn't looking at us; her eyes were on her computer screen. But I wasn't sure whether she was looking at anything. Of late, I had noticed that whenever Chloe and I talked, Jessie didn't quite take part. A few days later, when I pressed her for an answer, she said, "When you two talk about a problem, you guys perfectly understand each other, whereas you have to explain everything to me at least two to three times."

I didn't know what I could do to rectify the situation. I felt she was pulling away, and I didn't want that to happen. Although I wasn't sure whether Jessie liked me the way I did, I had a feeling she did too. *Maybe I should ask her out on a date.* We hadn't really defined our relationship yet. Since we had met again in that pub, it had been two months. I wanted to know how she felt about me.

Between my new job in R&D and our own project, I had totally forgotten about Lucy's visit that weekend. So when Jessie reminded me, "Lucy is coming home tomorrow morning," I knew what that meant. We needed to clear the mess we'd created when we had shifted everything to her room. But I had already had promised Chloe that I would help her study in the evening on surgical illnesses for her exam next week.

I had no choice but to postpone my tuition plan with Chloe. I walked up to her desk and said, "I'm sorry, Chloe, I can't do it tonight. I totally forgot I had something on."

"What am I supposed to do now? You know I have an exam next week, right?" She flared up.

"But this is something I had already promised earlier. Let's do it tomorrow."

"I can't. Tomorrow morning, I'm driving to Edmonton with my dad to my aunt's funeral. I'll be back on Sunday late afternoon. But hey, don't worry, you go do whatever you have to do," said Chloe, though she looked unhappy.

"Okay, okay, give me some time to sort this out. Let me cancel or postpone the other plan."

"I can't ask you to do that."

"Well, you aren't asking. It's my fault, and I'm going to fix it." I walked out to get some fresh air in the backyard. There was a small door in the study that led to the lawn at the back of the house. It was quiet out there. A huge oak tree covered most of the backyard, but it had a swing still hanging from one of its branches. I wanted to sit there, but I wasn't sure whether it would hold my weight. Suddenly, I heard Jessie's voice from behind me. "Go on, try it. Lucy and I had a great time here."

She slowly walked to the swing and sat by my side. She asked, "What were you guys arguing about?"

"Earlier I had promised Chloe to help her study this evening. I totally forgot about Lucy coming back this weekend."

"No biggie. Go help her study; I'll manage."

"Are you sure? Tell you what, I'll come back after we're done."

"Don't worry, I'm capable of moving some boxes." She leaned forward and kissed me.

Go on, ask her out now, a voice prompted me from inside my head. Sure, I was out of practice; I hadn't been on a date in a long time. I hadn't asked anyone out since I had asked Chloe about three years ago. And I was dying to know how Jessie felt about me. I said, "Jessie, would you like to—"

But before I got to the vital part, I was interrupted by Lukas. He called out from the window upstairs, "Where is my hot chocolate, Mom?"

"In a minute, sweetie," replied Jessie from the swing.

She turned to me and said, "Actually, I went to the kitchen to get the drinks. Then I saw you from the kitchen window, and I came out. This is his hot chocolate time. Anyway, don't mind him . . . go ahead, I'm listening." And she looked at me with her big blue eyes.

I looked her in the eye and asked, "Jessie, will you—" but Lukas interrupted again.

"Mom, I'm hungry," said Lukas. He had already come down the stairs and was standing at the back door.

Jessie looked at me, and I said, "Go ahead. We'll talk later."

After Jessie and Lukas went inside, I got up from the swing and paced up and down for a while. This was a big moment for me. The interruption was unfortunate, and I told myself to wait for the next opportune moment.

After a while, I went back to our office room to catch up with my work. Five minutes later, Jessie stepped in and asked, "Sorry about that. What did you want to ask me?"

Obviously, I didn't want to ask her out with Chloe in the same room. I said, "I forgot."

"You asked me whether I would like to do…what?" She tried to remind me.

I said, "Oh yeah, whether you would like to make coffee now?"

Jessie said, "Sure," with a slightly confused look, and she left.

Then I told Chloe that I had canceled the other plan, and I would help her study as we had planned.

"Thank you. Your place or mine?" asked Chloe.

"We can sit here if you want."

"Sorry, I don't have my books with me."

"Well, let's go to my place then. We'll pick up your books and some Chinese food on the way."

"Sure. As you wish, sir," said Chloe.

I felt bad to dump everything on Jessie again. It wasn't right. As it was, giving the room away for our work was a big favor. Clearing Lucy's room was the least I could've done.

Jessie left for her work after half an hour, and Chloe and I reached my place at about nine with some Chinese takeaway.

Chloe said, "Hey, your place still looks the same. May I use your bathroom? I don't want to use the small one; it makes me feel claustrophobic."

"Of course, please go ahead."

Chloe came back after five minutes, picked up her books, and sat on the sofa. Her face was pale, but then, she'd never used much makeup. When I asked her whether she wanted to eat first, she coldly said, "Not now."

I spoke non-stop for about twenty minutes on surgical illnesses, but I had no idea whether she was listening or not. Her gaze was fixed on the wall. Her eyes were icy-cold. "Anything else?" I asked to check.

"Nope, that's all . . . thank you."

"Do you want to eat now? I'm famished." I tried to lighten the mood. She hadn't said much since she had come back from the bathroom. I didn't know what had happened to her.

"You go ahead, I'm not hungry," answered Chloe.

"Well then, let me drive you home."

"Don't bother. You've done enough. I'll get a cab." And she left.

I felt a little uneasy. Did I do anything wrong? I waited outside the main gate as she got into a cab. I went inside to retrace the series of events as they had unfolded. I went to my bedroom and then to my bathroom. And soon I realized what must have had happened. She certainly hadn't expected to see makeup in my bathroom. And those weren't hers. She must've also noticed Jessie's dress hanging at the back of the door. The other day, Jessie had brought a change because she had an appointment the next morning, but I had forgotten all about that. Otherwise, I would've returned it to her. Still, I couldn't figure out why that should matter to Chloe. I had no idea what she had assumed, but I would've rather talked about it. Why would Jessie's spending a couple of nights at my place be such a crime? I wanted to scream at the top my voice, "Remember, we broke up?"

Chapter 9

I tossed and turned the whole night in my bed. *What did I do wrong?* The next day, I got up rather early and dragged myself to the living room. Even my favorite morning coffee failed to do its magic that day. God knew I had no intention to hurt Chloe. Having children after HD confirmation was a definite no-no for me, and we had broken up as soon as we found out about our differences. But did that mean I couldn't sleep with another woman in my lifetime? What about dating?

Thank god, I got a break from all the cacophony in my head as Jessie called me on her way back from the airport. I could hear her sister's voice in the car. "Your new boyfriend or what? Aren't you going to introduce me?"

"I'll…but can you shut up now?" Jessie retorted at her sister.

Although the chiding wasn't directed at me, after a bad night, I loved their warmth. I also wanted to join in the fun and tease her a little. I said, "Bad timing? Okay, I'll shut up now. Catch you later."

"Not you, silly, it's my stupid sister."

"Who are you calling stupid? Put your boyfriend on the speakerphone," demanded Lucy.

"David, can I call you back? I need to deal with my sister first." And she hung up. Or at least she thought she did. But I could still hear them.

"First off, he's not my boyfriend." Jessie's voice turned serious, "Honestly, I know nothing about this relationship yet. He has said nothing. He hasn't even asked me out."

"Ouch! That —" I heard Lucy's concerned voice, but I hung up. I didn't want to pry on Jessie; it was getting too personal.

Later that day, when I went to Jessie's house, she introduced me to her younger sister. I thanked Lucy for everything she had done for us. She was a vibrant, intelligent and cheerful girl in her mid-twenties. They looked like sisters, except Lucy was a brunette and preferred to wear glasses. Jessie said, "She thinks she looks intelligent with glasses."

"Hey, I am intelligent. I don't have to look like it," replied Lucy.

"Aren't you forgetting something? We have the same IQ," Jessie said.

I was surprised. I didn't know that. Maybe there were a lot of things about Jessie I still didn't know. I wanted to know them all, and I also didn't want to waste any more time. I had to ask her out as soon as possible. I came back to my senses as Mrs. James said, "Will you two stop this childish nonsense?" Then she asked me to have dinner with them.

When Jessie and I went to our new office room, I didn't see Chloe. On a regular day, she came around four in the afternoon. I looked at Jessie and asked, "What happened to Chloe?"

"Today is Saturday, David. Although she called me earlier and said she needed Monday and Tuesday off to study. I thought you knew as you were helping her," Jessie said.

"That didn't work out." And I told her what had happened the previous night.

Jessie apologized. "I shouldn't have left my stuff there; people might misunderstand."

"What's there to misunderstand? We are two consenting adults, and if you leave a few clothes at my place, I don't see how that can be anyone's business. Chloe has no right to be upset about anything. Chloe and I broke up more than six months ago, and it wasn't like one of us dumped the other one. It was mutual. We had irreconcilable differences, and we parted ways."

I got up from my chair and walked toward Jessie to say what I had been trying to say for the last twenty-four hours, but before I could open my mouth, Lucy pushed open the door and said, "Hey guys, I was thinking since I'll be here for another week or so, why don't we have an official meeting with all your overseas volunteers to outline the future—your visions, goals, and all that? The core team also gets to know each other. That's of course if you guys want to do it. I can set up a video conference."

I said, "That's great thinking, Lucy."

No wonder her company was paying her big bucks to pick her brain and had already drawn her into the management team. I said, "You're right. It will be nice to put a face to their names. Let's do it."

I added, "First, we need people to get tested for genetic diseases. The next step would be sharing our test results with others."

"But why do you want them to share their test results? Isn't that something very personal?" asked Lucy.

"Of course, it is. But this will also create a common bond between the victims and give them a platform to share their mutual problems. Think of it as any support group. And once we get a sizable public opinion from one area, we can go to that city and hold public workshops or seminars to motivate more people to take a decisive action. Of course, the local activists would have bigger roles to play."

"Shall I set it up for next Sunday evening?" asked Lucy. She sounded excited.

I looked at Jessie for her opinion, and she said, "Sure, let's do it."

However, within the next twenty-four hours, after the announcement went live, many volunteers requested us to shift the video conference to Saturday evening. People from Australia, New Zealand and other parts of the world in the east didn't want to miss their work on a Monday morning.

Lucy suggested a mock presentation amongst our team members in Calgary before we went live with the official presentation. She said, "This will put all of us here on the same page." We fixed the internal meeting for Friday. I wasn't too sure whether Chloe could make it, although her exam would be over by Tuesday. But when Jessie told Chloe about the new developments, she said she would be back to work on Wednesday, anyway.

We were bursting with excitement as we all gathered in Jessie's living room on Friday evening. I explained how a carrier screening test could be a real preventive measure for thousands of single-gene diseases and how a simple test could give thousands of parents their certificate of fitness. I said, "In fact, it's the only available practical solution. And the best part is now, with available at-home kits, you don't even have to go anywhere. Anyone can just take the blood sample and send it to a lab themselves for a carrier screening test. It's that simple. Preventive measures can work miracles. I'm sure we all remember what condoms have done to prevent HIV."

Once the presentation was over, Lucy said, "Yes, you guys are ready. I can't wait for tomorrow." Mrs. James served us muffins and apple pie. But then, Lucy asked us a question we had never thought of. "Have you guys considered getting funding? You need money to run this thing. I know you guys spend everything you earn on this, but trust me, going forward, it'll get even more expensive. You all need monthly remuneration, and I think you should pay your volunteers too. Your third-party costs and travel expenses will also shoot up soon."

We all sat back down. None of us had any clue how to get funding. Who would give us money to run this thing and why?

Lucy was the only corporate wizard among us. We looked at her, hoping she would show us the way. She said, "The first step would be to register yourself as a non-profit organization so that you would be ready to accept any donation when it comes your way. Don't you guys know anybody who could lead us to some sponsors?"

We all shook our heads. She said, "Well, based on your number of hits in the first few days, I can talk to a few companies for sponsorship." She paused for a minute and then continued. "You know what, hospitals and pharmaceutical companies will love these numbers."

Chloe had been sitting silently at one corner like the rest of us. Suddenly she said, "David could talk to Dr. Tyler. He loves him."

Lucy said, "I don't know this Dr. Tyler, but it may not be such a bad idea. When did you talk to him last, David?"

"Maybe a couple of months ago, before we had started the website. I saw him the other day, but we didn't talk much."

"Well, why don't you update him on your project and see what he has to say? You don't have to ask for money. If he's a wise man, he'll see the benefit for both parties here. And if he says nothing, I'll try to get you another hospital or a pharma company on board."

How does a twenty-three-year-old girl get to be so smart and confident about the whole world? Lucy had become a big-town girl; I had only heard about them and had never met one. Seeing her from such close proximity was an experience for me. You would never know what her sharp, penetrating eyes would demand next from behind those fashionable glasses.

The next morning, as I woke up, I wanted to curse Chloe for bringing up Dr. Tyler's name in that meeting. I had always hated to ask for anything. It left me with no choice but to see him as soon as possible. But a meeting had already been overdue, since I also had to thank him for the R&D job.

It turned out, Dr. Tyler was also happy to see me again. He said, "How are you, son? I haven't seen you for so long. Sorry about the other day for dumping everything on you—I was already running late. Now tell me what you've been up to."

I told him in detail what we had been doing in the last two and a half months. Then I opened my laptop and asked, "Do you have time to take a look at something?"

Dr. Tyler nodded, and I showed him the website. Dr. Tyler congratulated me and said, "How did you come up with that? You know what they say: the easiest answer is the most difficult to see." He patted me on the back and continued. "When you first told me about prevention, all I could think of was medicine, new R&D, gene alteration…that kind of thing. How silly? All along, the answer was right in front of our eyes. This is ingenious and brilliant."

"At first, I was thinking along those lines too," I admitted, and then I told him how Jessie came up with that idea.

"I must meet this lady: your girlfriend or what?"

"That's the thing. I don't know yet, sir."

"What are you talking about? You guys can solve such big problems and you two don't know whether you're in a relationship?"

I kept my head down. I didn't know how to answer that. But then he said something I had never expected of him. "I give you one week to tell her everything; otherwise, I'm going to tell her. It's you or me, and your time starts now."

We spent more than an hour together, and after seeing everything, Dr. Tyler said, "You may be on to something phenomenal there, David. You guys have achieved a lot within a short time. I'm very proud of you. Why don't you let the hospital be a part of this revolution? I can see something amazing happening soon. Indeed, one carrier screening test could be the answer. All along, the tricky part has been to get people to take the test. Now your awareness campaign can be a game changer."

I felt ecstatic. The best part was, I didn't even have to ask for anything. I remembered what Lucy had said the previous night, "It's like our need is another organization's public outreach." Dr. Tyler must have seen some value in our project for the hospital. He told me he would talk to the board soon and put me on to the PR guys.

Later, when I told the team about my conversation with Dr. Tyler, everybody cheered. I thanked Chloe for her suggestion. Lucy said, "See, it wasn't that difficult after all."

A while later, the team reconvened again in Jessie's living room for the video conference. We had over fifty-six log-ins when we started, and that number went up to seventy-two by the end of the session.

Two and a half hours later, when we turned off our computers, everyone agreed across the nations that until such time as viable cures or alternatives were found, the Parental Fitness Test should be our preventive pledge against all hereditary genetic diseases. I applauded Lucy. She had taken this fight to a whole new level. She politely said, "I did nothing; it was all you guys."

Still, I wanted to thank Lucy for everything she had done for us by treating her with a dinner the next day. I said, "My treat."

The next morning, my first job was to upload my genetic test results: HD positive. That was the beginning of our next big challenge—requesting people to come forward with their genetic disorders—declaring a silent war against all hereditary genetic diseases. Lucy said that, on the internet, everything was about numbers, so we'd just have to wait and see, hoping my one test result would soon be joined by others. But by seven in the evening, before we were leaving for the dinner, the number of test results posted had already swelled from one in the morning to two hundred and thirty-eight. People were rushing to share their genetic test results as if they had a vendetta against hereditary genetic disorders.

Later that night, Lucy packed her bag and left for Chicago. I had seen her up close for slightly more than a week, but it felt like we had known each other for a long time. I felt a unique connection with her, maybe for two reasons. One, she was Jessie's sister, and two, for her contributions to our project, for the way she'd jumped in—heart and soul. She was super-busy, yet she found time to help. An amazing girl.

Jessie, Chloe, and I drove Lucy to the airport. The ride together was good fun; they even sang along with the radio. But on our way back, we all went silent. I drove all the way without anyone saying a word. We all missed Lucy's presence. First, I dropped Chloe off, and ten minutes later, I pulled up in front of Jessie's house.

Jessie unbuckled herself, kissed me goodnight, and was half-way out when I suddenly pulled her back in by one hand and said, "Will you go out on a date with me?"

Jessie looked at me and said, "What took you so long?" and kissed me. Then, she hugged me and whispered from behind my back, "Of course. Of course, I will."

I would never forget the Saturday night that followed. I was so excited that I couldn't sleep the night before. In the last few days of that week, I had announced my date with Jessie to almost everyone I met—Dr. Tyler, my mom, Mrs. James, Uncle Tom, my mom's neighbor, and Eliza at my regular diner—everyone except one person. After the sharp reaction from Chloe the other day, I couldn't bring myself to tell her about my date with Jessie. I didn't know how she would react this time, and I didn't want to bring out any unpleasantness anywhere. I decided to tell her later at the right moment.

Finally, the much-anticipated Saturday night arrived. My heart had been beating fast all day. Jessie looked incredibly nice in a short black dress and ankle boots. She never had to do anything with her hair. It looked drop-dead gorgeous as it was, a long bob with side bangs. Although I had not seen her using much makeup since I had met her in the pub, that night, she must have made it a point to show what a difference it would make if she ever gave it a go again. I almost couldn't recognize her as she came down the stairs. "You look great," I blurted out in a dazed voice.

"That's my Jessie," said Mrs. James with a big grin on her face, still standing at the door.

I had already booked a table for two at Le Méridien. However, the first few minutes of the date seemed really awkward. I was completely out of practice, and I didn't even know what to say. We knew each other so well that small talk became superfluous. So instead of asking non-relevant, foolish questions, I asked her something that had been puzzling me for the last few days. Recently, from Lucy's comment, I had found out Jessie wasn't the kind of stupid she had acted in school. In fact, she seemed to have a really high IQ, so I asked, "Why did you act so stupid in school to where you could never do your homework?"

"Why do you think, silly?"

"I have no idea."

"I couldn't have talked to you about the weather or our cheerleading, right? And I was lazy too. I liked you a lot back then, so I thought it would be a little bit of me time." Jessie paused for a while. "Besides, do you know that I could've been a geek? I had seen intelligent students being bullied by classmates all the time, and I decided to beat them in their own game."

"Didn't anyone suspect anything?" I asked.

"Did you? Blondes are considered dumb. I just played along." And she smiled.

"But why didn't you say anything to me?" I asked naively.

"Are you crazy or what? That would've been social suicide for me. Please don't be mad at me."

"How can I not be mad at you? You lied to me." At first, I wanted to tease her a little. But when I looked at her sad face, I couldn't continue the act. I said, "I was joking. No harm done. You're in the clear, Jessie."

She smiled, but her smile faded as fast as it came.

"What's wrong?" I asked.

"I guess you're right. I lied to everyone. And they're all having the last laugh now. I lost out in the last game…I'm a loser," Jessie said in a solemn voice.

"Who said you're a loser?"

"Look at me, David. I am almost twenty-nine, and what do I do for a living? … Bartending. Ha-ha, if that's not a joke, what is?" Jessie looked at me.

"But don't you think campaigning for carrier screening tests is worth doing?"

"I didn't say it wasn't. Of course, it is. This is probably the best thing that has happened to me in a long time."

"Now you're exaggerating." I tried to lighten the mood.

I knew my date with Jessie wouldn't be the regular kind, but I didn't expect it to turn out so overwhelmingly personal. I was glad I had asked her out, though. In one evening, I got to know her ten times better, and I caught up on everything I had missed out in all those years. As Jessie settled in, she told me what she had gone through since high school. It was a turbulent ride for any twenty-year-old woman. Back then she had been dating a senior named Dylan Miller. When Dylan first proposed to marry her, Mrs. James had said they were too young to get married, but young minds never listened to sensible words, so they had eloped to Vegas and got married.

Jessie said, "His father came to work in Canada, and that's how Dylan landed in our school. Do you remember a guy on our soccer team with a British accent? ... Redhead, tall, and well-built?" She tried her best to help me remember if I had ever seen a guy like that.

"Sorry, Jessie . . . doesn't ring a bell." I gave up.

"Anyway, it's not important. When Dylan was in his third-year of college, his father's tenure ended here and his parents left. They insisted on him going back too. But I asked Dylan to finish his studies here, and I took a full-time job after school graduation. Thankfully, Dylan's father still paid for his tuition fees, but we were young, and our expenses were high. My job wasn't paying enough to sustain that lifestyle." Jessie looked sad.

"Stop it. What's the point in talking about all this? I don't want to know your past. I am more than happy with the present."

"I know. But I want you to know everything."

"Don't worry about it. Maybe later someday when you're more ready to talk about it."

I didn't want our date to turn into a fact-finding mission. Of course, I wanted to get to know her, but knowing her also could be about her present and her future plans. *What does she want in life?* I would've loved to know how she felt about me. *Where do I figure in her plans?*

I didn't get the answers to those questions that day, but we had a good time. Jessie was a great conversationalist. She could impersonate anyone; she took out her glasses from her bag and mimicked our principal. She narrated some other high school stories as well. Sadly, the last time Jessie had had any fun was in her high school days—that's why all her stories revolved around the school days. But I loved to hear those stories.

Chapter 10

"Meet me for lunch today," said Dr. Tyler when he called me on the phone a week later. I presumed it was about his meeting with the board. I was dying to know the outcome. We met in his office at one in the afternoon, and we headed for the cafeteria. But before we entered, Dr. Tyler said, "Forget the cafeteria. Let's do something different today. You want a steak?"

The truth was, I wasn't thinking about any food that day. Not that I wasn't hungry, but I was more eager to know the board's decision. A lot was depending on that. But I looked at him and said, "Steak is great, sir."

Next to our hospital, there was a small, family-run steakhouse in the mall. Once we walked in, it became clear to me that Dr. Tyler was a known customer there. Maggie, the owner's wife, smiled at him and showed us to a quiet table at one corner. I didn't know whether that was an unspoken arrangement between both parties. Perhaps the owner had assumed it was an important meeting. If a busy doctor simply wanted to have lunch, he would've eaten at the hospital cafeteria.

The steak was nice but even nicer was what Dr. Tyler had to say. "The hospital board is thrilled with your revolutionary thinking and would like to be a part of this movement. Your PowerPoint presentation was absolutely to the point and they loved it." He paused. Then, he asked, "Didn't you say you have a finance guy on your team?"

"She is Jessie's younger sister, Lucy. She isn't exactly a finance person per se, but she works as a project manager in a software company in Chicago."

"Well, can you get in touch with her?"

"Sure, sir. What do you have in mind?" I was almost sitting on the edge of my chair.

"Get us your projected annual expenditures for the next three years. Consider this: Jessie and you may have to go full-time, so take that compensation into account. We don't want you guys to waste time anywhere else. Also, make provisions for hourly payments to good volunteers; they need to eat too. We want everyone's heart and soul—their best."

"But we aren't doing this for money, sir. We strongly feel, together, we can stop this."

"My sentiments exactly. This is a massive project, David. You need to convince people, and you must reach out to as many obstetricians and gynecologists as possible to motivate them to offer carrier screening tests in the preconception period. To move anything forward, you need people, and people need money. But people without passion achieve nothing. You guys mentioned that you might be ready to have your first seminar or workshop in one year, right?"

I nodded.

"With resources, we can possibly make it happen in six months, or maybe sooner."

Everything Dr. Tyler said made sense. He was the one person in the world I'd always trusted. He was also a very influential person in the hospital. He always believed there were two things needed to get to the top: merit and hard work. Not that he never had enemies—I had heard that he'd even kicked out a trustee's son once for malpractice—, but his detractors were always outnumbered by his supporters.

After work, I drove to Jessie's house as fast as I could. I called everyone to the living room and told them verbatim what Dr. Tyler had said. Mrs. James got up first and pulled everyone together for a group hug. Lukas slipped in the middle and put his arms around Jessie. The news overwhelmed everyone; it was finally happening. But soon we came back to our senses as Lukas screamed out, "I can't breathe, Mom," and we quickly disentangled ourselves.

Once we went back to our small office, I thanked Chloe for thinking of Christchurch as a sponsor. I also admitted, "On my own, I would've never thought of asking Dr. Tyler for such help."

"I did nothing, David. It was all you," Chloe answered calmly. Things between Chloe and me had been a little awkward since she had stormed out of my house that night. I hoped someday she would understand that I had no intention of hurting her, but I couldn't keep my life on hold forever.

Later that evening, we arranged a teleconference with Lucy to discuss what Dr. Tyler had said. She congratulated me for two things: for getting Dr. Tyler on board so fast and for taking her sister out on a date. She also promised to send a revised financial plan by the weekend.

I soon realized what that second part of the congratulation would mean to Chloe. After the meeting, she picked up her bag and left. I was given no opportunity to talk to her. I cursed myself for not mentioning the date to her earlier. I was waiting for the right time, but it had blown up right in my face. Jessie also noticed the abrupt change in Chloe's behavior. She asked, "What's up with her?"

"I don't know. But I'm going to find out."

"I'm guessing you didn't tell her we went out, right?"

I nodded and tried to finish my work. Yet all I could see was Chloe's face in front of me. *But what else could I have done? I didn't know how she would react.* Anyway, I called it a day and went to meet her at her house.

Chloe's father, Mr. Clayton, opened the door and invited me in. He worked in a law firm and had always maintained a busy schedule. Unlike Chloe, he dressed formally even while at home. The first time I had met him three years ago, I thought he was about to go out; that day, Chloe had laughed and said, "That's the way my father dresses when he's at home. Get used to it."

Mr. Clayton had already poured himself a glass of wine, and from the look of the dining table, I figured he had been working. He had his laptop open and some papers scattered all over the table. That was the second thing Chloe had mentioned about him in our first meeting. "He is always working." Indeed, I had spent so much time in that house in the last three years, yet I had never seen him watching TV or doing anything else like other parents normally did.

"Come in, David. What a pleasant surprise! Wine?"

"Well, maybe one."

"Come tell me what you have been up to." Mr. Clayton had heard from Chloe how much I'd wanted to be a heart surgeon. And he had also heard how that life-changing interview of mine had ended. He said, "The hospital can't refuse you the job just because you're HD positive. You know that, right?"

But I was in no mood to go through that all over again. "They offered me the job, sir, but I opted for R&D instead." I paused and asked, "Is Chloe around? I need to talk to her."

"She's in her room upstairs," answered Mr. Clayton.

Chloe's door was half open, so I knocked.

"Come in, Dad, but I'm not hungry. You go ahead." Chloe's eyes were still on her computer screen. I stood in front of the door, confused. I knocked again and said, "Hi! It's me."

I guess my voice surprised Chloe quite a bit. She took a sudden turn and nearly fell from her chair. I said, "I didn't mean to startle you. I'm sorry. You jumped like you saw a ghost."

"Duh! Anybody would be startled by a stupid ex-boyfriend."

"Well, 'ex' I can understand, but 'stupid'?"

"What did you think? You would date someone under my nose, and I would never find out?"

"That wasn't my intention. I'm sorry you had to find out that way. I was looking for the right opportunity. I didn't know how to tell you."

"Why?" She looked me in the eye.

"I thought you would be upset and wouldn't approve."

"I'm upset all right, but who am I to approve? Frankly, I'm not angry with you or with Jessie; I'm angry with myself. I had my chances, and I blew it. So, no, I have no right to be upset. I want my mind to accept that. Go ahead, date Jessie as much as you want. She's a lucky girl." And she rushed to the bathroom.

After some time, she asked from the bathroom in a broken voice, "Is there anything else?"

"Not really." And I left the room after waiting for a few minutes.

Chloe had always been a sensitive girl. She was hurt, but unfortunately, I had no idea how I could be of any help. At first, when I had met her again at Dr. Tyler's office, I assumed a frank conversation with her would set me free. *There's nothing that an open dialogue between two adults can't fix.* But instead, it had opened a Pandora's Box. Maybe, for once, I would have been better off with no knowledge, or at least less of it.

But I was still struggling with one question. Why had Chloe agreed to volunteer for us in the first place? Did she feel sorry for me, and she wanted to help in any way she could? Or did she want to help us to advance her resume? Or did she secretly think working there might bring us back together? Unfortunately, only Chloe had the answers.

Lucy kept her promise and sent me the financial project report for the next three years by Monday morning. For all I knew, she could've worked all Sunday and throughout the night, but there was no mention of any of that, and I had enough to ponder as it was. I thanked her in a reply email and rushed to Dr. Tyler's office.

Dr. Tyler's chamber was much bigger than the other doctors' offices in our hospital because he had many meetings going on in his room all the time. He also had an efficient secretary as his gatekeeper. However, this time, I had an appointment; besides, she also knew me as one of his favorite students.

"Good morning, sir," I greeted him to draw his attention. He had been looking out, standing in front of the window. *Very unusual.* In the last seven years that I had known him, I'd never thought he had time for such things.

He greeted me all right, but I sensed something off. I asked, "What's wrong, sir?"

"Well, I don't know how to put it; the hospital board has now reversed its decision. There's a sentiment among some board members that promoting a mandatory carrier screening test before having children might get the wrath of some religious groups. You know how sensitive that would be for us, right?"

Christchurch was a missionary hospital, and running a non-profit division devoted to what many saw as a moral and religious concern could be tricky. *Why didn't I think of that?*

"Of course, sir, I understand. Don't worry about it. We'll find some other ways and continue working on it. I'll keep you posted."

Deep in my heart, I knew we had suffered a major blow. I felt most for Lucy; she had put in a lot of work toward it. In a way, we were all looking forward to it. Not that any of us were thinking of making drastic lifestyle changes with fat salaries, but it had brought hope to our volunteers, and as Dr. Tyler had said earlier, it could also expedite everything.

The human mind works in a peculiar way. Although we had suffered no material loss, the loss of hope brought me down that evening. But that also made me realize why so many people from all over the world had latched onto this fight: it was hope. They had seen a ray of hope to stop all the inherited genetic diseases. *Who knows, if we are successful in our campaign, it might be the "eureka" moment in fighting all single-gene diseases.* But I knew I had to hurry.

I was still thinking about what Dr. Tyler had said just before I left: "I love your carrier screening test awareness program, because this will always be the first step in stopping single-gene diseases—even after editing the DNA of a human embryo becomes legally available everywhere."

I called Lucy to break the bad news to her myself. She calmly said, "Don't worry about it. We'll get another sponsor. Now isn't the time to lose hope. So, you guys do your thing, and I'll go look for a sponsor. I guess we have to work harder."

I felt good after talking with Lucy. I loved her confidence in the project. Five minutes later, when Jessie came in, I said, "Let's forget Christchurch. We still need to spread our stories as fast as possible. Like in all fatal diseases, this is also a race against time. One day early means thousands of fewer fatalities."

I needed to say those words out loud to remain strong. The good thing was the total number of members was still growing, and we were hoping those who had already consented to a carrier screening test could convince their friends, and then, their friends' friends. Of course, the hospital's help would have been great, but we couldn't stop just because they weren't able to participate. We had to move on, no matter what.

Two days later, Lucy made an unexpected stop for the weekend. Jessie told me she used to do that a lot at first when she'd moved to Chicago. But with time, she got busier, and she'd stopped coming home as often unless she had some work to do here. Mrs. James sounded happy. "With your Toronto project, at least we see you more often now."

I was also happy to see her again. And, being the wise person Lucy was, she made an interesting suggestion: "Why don't we put up the request for sponsorship on our site and share the proposal with others?"

Jessie argued, "But how is that going to help? We can't ask our members for money."

"We aren't asking for anything. Since the proposal is ready, we can also share it with them like we shared our vision board. The thing is, sometimes vision boards need monetary support to reach their goals. Who knows, one of them may have the right contacts?"

Putting it up on our website was worth a shot. "It might not be such a bad idea," I tried to explain to Jessie. "After all, the same proposal made Christchurch interested. Who knows, there might be another hospital or insurance company waiting to do a similar thing?"

I didn't want to think about the alternative yet. Going on our own would definitely make fundraising a regular event, and we couldn't expect Lucy doing it for us. From the three-year projection report, I had realized we would require a lot of money for our travel expenses and workshops and seminars.

However, as I went back to the office on Monday morning, my colleague, Jonathon said, "Dr. Tyler came looking for you."

That was a little odd. I had never seen him in our building before. So I rushed to his office. From our R&D Division to the main hospital building, it was a clear seven minutes' walk. I didn't mind the walk, but I wondered why he hadn't left me a message. The anxiety was killing me. Was it something to do with my illness, or did he simply want to say "Hello"? I hadn't seen him in the last few days since the hospital authorities pulled out.

When I reached his office, he had already left for the operation room. Alice told me he wouldn't be back until lunchtime and that she would try to squeeze me in. Unfortunately, he couldn't meet me even at lunchtime. I heard the operation ran into multiple complications, and Dr. Tyler didn't finish until quite late in the evening.

I didn't have a great day either. I felt restless the whole day. I still didn't know why he had come looking for me. And above everything else, why didn't he leave me a message? Of late, I had also realized I didn't like going to his office anymore. It reminded me of everything I had given up. The frequent visits to Dr. Tyler's office and the regular chit-chats with my ex-colleagues in corridors or at the cafeteria about their daily routines made it impossible for me to ignore what I was missing. And every time I visited Dr. Tyler's office, it was like walking on my shattered dreams. It pained me immensely as I crossed the Hall of Fame, but otherwise, I had to take an even longer walk.

I came back home pretty depressed. *Did I do the right thing by declining the heart surgeon's job?* Otherwise, it could've been me there in that operating room. But then again, all that would have been so uncertain. What if Dr. Tyler's message was about my HD? Could that be the reason he wanted to talk face-to-face?

No report could've told me when my symptoms would appear or how long I could delay the onset of the disease. Nothing was up to me. Every time I dropped my keys or I toppled something accidentally, I shivered in fear. I looked closely at my fingers to check any abnormal movements. I was living like a fish in a lake, swimming around with fishermen closing in from all sides. The inevitable was coming, but I didn't know when. And that was killing me.

Perhaps I would never know for sure that I had made the right decision until the day I fell sick. And, until then, I would be miserable.

The next day, when I finally met Dr. Tyler in the hallway, I congratulated him on the complicated heart surgery.

"You know what, David, I still can't believe you aren't operating. I miss you in the operating room."

"I miss that too, sir."

"Maybe it's not too late yet; if you want, I can still talk to the board."

"But I have taken on something, sir, and a lot of people are now depending on me. Although I don't know what will happen next."

"That's true; you're on to a much bigger thing now. Forget I mentioned surgery. And about that, come, let's go to my room."

Once again, I walked across the Hall of Fame with Dr. Tyler, but this time, I didn't feel so demoralized. Dr. Tyler said, "You might be on to something really big. This might change the lives of millions of people."

I smiled at Alice as I walked past her, and Dr. Tyler asked her to send two coffees inside. From Dr. Tyler's conversations, I had already assumed it was about the parental fitness test program and not about my health. But I was getting impatient, so as soon as we entered the room, I asked, "Did you want to talk about the project?"

"Yes, David. A foundation run by a European pharmaceutical company is interested. They're doing a lot of research on drugs for genetic diseases, and they're willing to fund your awareness campaign for carrier screening tests."

Dr. Tyler gave me all the necessary details and told me about his association with the "big bosses," who happened to be his long-time friends. However, he asked me to check their website for more updated information.

"That's great news, sir. It seems this will be quite in line with their work."

"Exactly. They feel the same way, too. This will help grow awareness of genetic diseases. I'll set up the first meeting for you in New York, and if all goes well, then you might have to fly to their headquarters in Zurich."

"I can't thank you enough, sir."

"I did nothing, David. I showed them what you guys have done, and they liked it."

As I left Dr. Tyler's office, I took out my phone to call Jessie. However, before I could make the call, I bumped into Chloe in the main lobby. In her white residency coat, I almost couldn't recognize her. She asked, "Hey, how are you doing? What are you doing here?"

"I came to see Dr. Tyler."

"Haven't they pulled out of the program already?" she asked in a concerned tone.

"Yes, they did, but Dr. Tyler has found another prospect for us."

"Tell me more about it. Coffee? I also need to tell you something." And Chloe walked toward the cafeteria.

When we sat down in one corner with our coffee, I said, "You go first."

"No way," Chloe protested. "Yours is much bigger news."

I repeated what Dr. Tyler had just told me. After hearing everything, she said, "It seems like a nice fit. Sounds like a done deal to me."

"I am hopeful. We'll see." Then, I asked her what she wanted to discuss.

"I don't think I can volunteer there anymore. At first, I thought I could do it, but it drains me. Besides, my exams are coming up too," Chloe said in a solemn voice.

"I understand," I said.

"I hope you don't mind. I am sorry for making a scene the other day. I wish you guys good luck."

Before I could say anything, Chloe got up and said, "I gotta go now. I'm assisting Dr. Herbert in the operating room," and she left.

I wasn't sure whether she rushed for the operation, or she didn't want another emotional breakdown. I felt sad for her, but I also knew I could do nothing. Maybe she was right: time away from us might help her heal faster. I decided not to call Jessie. Instead, I'd wait until the evening to give her the news. My conversation with Chloe had squeezed the excitement out of me, and I took a slow walk back to the lab.

Chapter 11

One month later, Chloe's prediction came true. Our first meeting with the pharmaceutical company in New York City went through without a hitch. Thank god, I had the two sisters by my side that day. And ten days later, Jessie and I flew to Zurich to make everything official.

I hadn't posted any news about the new funding possibilities on our website yet because I wanted to be one hundred percent sure before announcing it to the whole world again. I had learned a hard lesson before in the Christchurch Hospital case—anything could happen. However, I mentioned our visit in an email to Tom, Mika, Theo, and Jennifer, a few very active volunteers in Berlin. I wanted to be ready for the next course of action if everything turned out as planned in Zurich. I told them that Jessie and I would be in Zurich and that we would like to meet them in Berlin after we had finished our work.

I didn't know what Dr. Tyler or the company people in the New York office had told the big bosses about us in Switzerland, but they gave us the VIP treatment. We didn't have to sell them anything; they had already decided to go ahead. Our presence seemed strictly ceremonial. They were moved because Jessie and I were both victims of genetic diseases. They liked the fact that we had built this movement based on real people and real-life stories. Thus, the passion and the urge to embrace carrier screening tests came across as real and genuine to them. The facts were overwhelming, they said, and the figures just helped.

We finished our work in Zurich within two days—with a visit to their cutting-edge research facility in Basel and meetings back-to-back. Zurich was a beautiful city, but we had no time to see or visit any place except Lake Zurich. We spent most of our time next to the lake, right in the heart of Zurich's financial district. The Albis and the Zimmerberg Hills in the south and the Pfannenstiel Hills on the north made the forty-kilometer long Lake Zurich a scenic beauty day and night. But I would never forget the view of the lake I had one evening from their conference room—the tiny lights from the houses piercing through the forested hills all around the lake made the composition look like a huge necklace with pieces of diamonds in it. As I stood there in awe by the huge glass window, Dr. Edgar pointed to one part of the lake and said, "That's 'Golden Coast,' and those houses and villas on the hills are some of the most expensive jewels in Switzerland. Care to get one, David?"

I looked at him and smiled, thinking I wouldn't mind spending a few nights with Jessie there. Although our hosts wanted us to stay the weekend and go sightseeing, we told them we would rather get started and meet our team in Germany instead. And obviously, they couldn't say "no."

But I didn't miss the sightseeing as much as I missed something much more important. I wanted to take Jessie to a restaurant by the lakeside, but we didn't have time. On our way back to the airport, as we were crossing the Limmat River, I showed her the restaurant from the bridge and apologized for not being able to make that happen.

But Jessie had a quick reply. "I'll only accept your apology if you promise me something in return."

"What's that?"

"That, someday, you will bring me here for dinner."

I didn't know how, but I knew I would love to make that happen. I said, "Yes, I promise." I wished she knew I wanted to promise her much more. If it were up to me, I would've taken her to the Alps at that very moment and would've shouted "I love you" from the top of the cliffs, leaving behind the echoes to reverberate perpetually in the air. But how could I? Wouldn't that be wrong? I had been asking myself the same questions over and over, and every time, a voice inside my head reminded me, "Hold on, you have HD."

We reached Berlin around midday on a Saturday. We had less than a day in hand. I needed to go back to my office on Monday morning. I was new to the organization, and we were in the middle of an important project, so my boss had been reluctant to give me any leave of absence. When he had agreed to let me go for Thursday and Friday, I'd considered that a great favor.

Berlin was a vibrant city, so even though we went no-where to explore the city, we felt the energy everywhere—from weekend farmers' market to crowded bistros and cafés.

Tom and Mika lived in a nice apartment at Kollwitz-platz. Mika had left her job about four years before when their daughter, Christine, was diagnosed with Marfan syndrome. The disease had already affected most of her connecting tissues from head to toe. She had lost her usual strength and flexibility in bones and muscles, ligaments and blood vessels. Her heart valves had also become very weak. She had been suffering from perpetual shortness of breath, causing her continuous fatigue and heart palpitations. Other than that, Christine was like any eleven-year-old kid, only a lot slender. But what struck me most about Christine was her smile, and I guess that had a lot to do with her parents' attitude toward her illness. Their world revolved around her. They wouldn't take part in anything—social or otherwise—if they had to do it without Christine.

Mika said, "We know we have to live by a different set of rules. I had left my job, and I'm a stay-home mom now. But when I first looked at your website, I wanted to volunteer. I thought this could be my way of contributing to society. After all, I have a first-hand nursing experience of Marfan syndrome for the last four years." Her face looked sad but resolved.

"Absolutely. All of us can bring immense value to the movement from our own experiences." Jessie grabbed Mika's hand in a show of solidarity.

One by one, the rest of the team members arrived, and the meeting turned out to be quite a gathering. The excitement was running high, and the moment we told them about the real purpose of our visit to Zurich, all hell broke loose. Mika's husband, Tom, popped open a bottle of champagne to celebrate the occasion.

"Dear friends, we got the funding. Now it's official. Their support will help us grow faster," I announced.

They all raised their glasses and screamed, "Cheers for PFT." We didn't even know when the Parental Fitness Test had become PFT there. I looked at Jessie, and she smiled with a shrug.

I also told them that after the initial formalities were over, we should work on our much-needed workshops to help campaign locally. "We need more people on board for carrier screening tests. Remember, not everyone will be convinced. Many may oppose due to their personal and religious beliefs, but that doesn't make them our enemies. Over time, we can win them over."

We left the Eurozone under Tom, Mika, Theo, and Jennifer's care, and Jessie and I boarded a flight back home on Sunday morning.

On Monday morning, before going to the lab, I ran to Dr. Tyler's office to update him on our Zurich trip and how some of our immediate plans had developed in Europe. Dr. Tyler said, "I'm glad you guys have found a strong base in Berlin. This will help you spread the word in Europe."

Finally, what Jessie and I had started a couple of months before—to test how the other parents felt about parental fitness tests—had turned into a full-blown movement. After coming back, the first thing on our agenda was to look for a small office space in Calgary. Although Mrs. James had never complained about giving up her study, and she'd always seemed more than happy that we ran our office from her house, we couldn't take her generosity for granted.

Later that week when I submitted my resignation to my R&D boss, I was more than surprised the way he reacted. He wasn't particularly a friendly guy; he was more like a stickler for rules. I had to serve two weeks' notice as per my terms of employment, though I would have loved to get an early release. I didn't know how, but I got my wishes granted. My boss said, "We'll miss you, David, but if you want to leave early, you can hand over your stuff to Michelle." *How did that happen? Had Dr. Tyler got anything to do with that too?*

Just when I thought everything was going well, I got a jolt from Jessie one evening later that week. During the last few days, we hadn't had any time to talk about us. There were no romantic dinners or movie dates; all we ever talked about was our project. But I had always thought we were standing on solid grounds. That was until Jessie dropped a bomb that evening.

"My ex-husband, Dylan, came by again last night," said Jessie.

"What do you mean by 'again'? You mean after four years?"

"Not really. He first came back last week when we were in Europe."

"How come you didn't tell me about that until now?"

"Because I didn't think he would come back. Anyway, he came again last night, and he's in town for three more days."

"What does he want?"

"He wants Lukas back in his life. He wants shared custody. He said, after all, we weren't legally divorced; he would love to patch things up between us, and blah, blah, blah."

Suddenly, I didn't know what to say or what to think anymore. Jessie had already told me that Dylan hadn't signed the divorce papers. They had been lying ready in her drawer for a long time. I had always thought it was a simple matter of formality. But after what Jessie had said, I wasn't so sure anymore. I blurted out, "What do you want?"

"You know what I want. But I have to think about my son, too. He needs a father in his life, right?"

"Right." And I pulled out a jacket from the stand.

"Where are you going?" asked Jessie, bewildered.

"I need a drink."

"Can I come?"

"I think I need some time alone."

But as I stepped out, I didn't want to go for a drink anymore; instead, I drove back home. I sat down and remembered what Jessie had just said.

I hated the way I had reacted. What was I thinking? I had acted like a teenage lover. Jessie and her son needed a family, and who was better equipped to fulfill that commitment? Dylan or an HD victim?

I felt terribly embarrassed for my emotional outburst. I didn't know why, but for the next few days, my first instinct was to avoid meeting Jessie. Suddenly, I didn't know what to say to her anymore. And whenever we met, I sat there quietly, as if I was lost for words.

But I soon realized that I couldn't let my feelings affect our work. We had more important things to do. People were looking to us for direction, and we now had to report to the funding oversight committee. Besides, I didn't have the luxury to waste time; I didn't even know how much time I had.

Fortunately, the tsunami of new problems that came in the wake of renting a small office space on the second floor of a small building in town swept us off our feet. It made me realize I wouldn't survive this if I couldn't separate my emotions from work.

However, we could have avoided all those new, office-related hassles if we had agreed to operate out of Toronto, because our sponsor company already had available office space in downtown Toronto.

But Jessie was stumped when she had first heard about it. "Toronto?" She repeated after me in disbelief. She said, "I can't leave Lukas alone at home in Toronto. My mother looks after him for more than twelve hours a day here. And my mother has a job in Calgary, so she can't go."

We sat down and decided to do whatever necessary to work from Calgary. We got the interior work done, bought new furniture, and shifted all our office stuff from Jessie's house. Within one week, we were all set. Meanwhile, we had also hired a lady named Melissa to assist us in filling the administrative vacuum building up since Chloe had left us. Melissa had worked in Toronto as a clinical program coordinator, providing support to children and their families throughout their care experience. She was a perfect fit. In fact, Melissa was our first paid assistant. Although she had been born and brought up in Toronto, she had moved to Calgary a year ago when her husband had taken a lecturer's job at Calgary University.

It took us three more days to set up the new network. By then, Melissa had had time to familiarize herself with our work. Jessie and I were responsible for Canada and the US markets. The Eurozone was gaining traction, and they were getting much better responses than we had done locally. I told Jessie, "Maybe workshops can help. We are far behind the Europe numbers."

Jessie agreed. "I'll start working on it, but first, we have to make a short trip to Seattle this weekend."

In the last few months, on her own, Jessie had made some progress in the Seattle, Washington DC, and New York City areas. Melissa pulled out all our recent communications with the Seattle volunteers to bring us up to speed.

But all our plans changed when the secretary of Dr. Roger Edward, the big boss in our sponsor's NYC office, called and told me to be in New York that weekend. At first, I feared the worst. Were they pulling the plug? That would be so unfair. We had just got started.

But it turned out I worried for nothing. It was the annual bash at Dr. Edward's beach house at the Hamptons. Apparently, everyone who knew Dr. Edward was supposed to know about that party as well, since it happened every year.

But once we reached there, the party looked like a movie set to me. I had never been to that kind of gathering in my life—maybe that was how the rich socialized and showed off their opulence. As we entered, I saw the car park packed with expensive cars and limos. The huge mansion was teeming with people. The crowd spilled over to a huge lawn at the back, facing the sea. *What a view!* I stood there for a minute to breathe and reassure myself that I was alive and not dreaming. Champagne flowed like tap water, with caviar, smoked salmon, and cream cheese arranged on trays on every table. A beautiful fragrance filled the air with "Mwah…mwah" echoing every now and then. It was one of those parties where everyone knew everyone, which made me wonder why he had invited us. I couldn't get my head around that.

He had said "hello" to us once when we had entered, but he hadn't spoken another word with us since then, save to introduce us to his daughter, Mia, and to tell us to enjoy ourselves. Mia was in her early twenties and was also a great host. There was no Mrs. Edward though; Mia told us her mother had passed away on her sixteenth birthday. I felt her father had given Mia more than she could handle. She was running around from one group to another to make sure everyone was enjoying the party.

However, I still felt jittery about the whole thing. It was obvious we didn't belong there, and we had nothing do with that party. It was a total waste of time for us, but Jessie said we needed to stick around.

Moments later, Jessie and Mia started discussing fashion. The men and women around them, wearing designer clothing, must have brought it on. That was another good thing about Jessie; she could talk to anyone about anything. *When does she have time to read about fashion these days?* Yet she seemed very well-informed.

I still felt it had been a waste of time, and I wanted to leave the party. I excused myself and walked toward the main building in search of the host himself. However, halfway to the mansion, I heard the loud sound of a chopper landing, and I saw Dr. Edward rushing out of the mansion and walking toward the helipad. *That must be some important guest. Well, so much for my efforts.* I stood there for a while, and then, as I turned back to go join Jessie, I heard someone calling out my name. I turned around and saw Dr. Edward with a rather familiar face—a tall gentleman with broad shoulders. He looked to be in his late forties. Had I seen him somewhere?

"The US Senator Robert Ruth!" I gulped. *What is he doing here?*

"Just the man I was looking for," said Dr. Edward. But I wasn't sure why he was looking in my direction.

I turned around, thinking I was blocking someone important. But to my surprise, there was no one behind me. Was I the man he was looking for? But why?

He pulled me closer to Senator Ruth and said, "This is the guy I was talking about. David, Senator Ruth. Senator Ruth, David."

Never mind the brief introduction, I was more puzzled by what he'd said first. God knows why he talked about me to Senator Ruth. I was going out of my wits.

Senator Ruth extended his right arm to shake hands with me. "Hello, David. Dr. Edward told me all about you and—"

But Dr. Edward interrupted. "Let's go to the library and get comfortable there."

"Sure," said the senator, and he followed Dr. Edward.

I followed them, too, along with two dark-suited bodyguards. *Why do they always have to wear dark glasses?* But I didn't have time to think about his security guys. My curiosity was killing me. Apparently, Dr. Edward hadn't invited us here without any purpose, but he also hadn't told us anything about a meeting with a senator. I had almost zero knowledge about corporate America. I had lived all my life in a sleepy town in Canada. All this was pretty much like a fantasy world to me.

"Where is Jessie?" asked Dr. Edward, and I came back to my senses.

"She's on the lawn with Mia. Shall I get her?" I would have loved to get some air and get Jessie's view on all this. She might have a clue about what was going on.

But Dr. Edward stopped me and instead asked one of his errand boys to find Jessie. "Tell her it's important. We'll be waiting for her in the library."

Five minutes later, as we settled down into the big library room upstairs, Senator Ruth looked at me and said, "Edward tells me you've undertaken a massive task. I appreciate your generosity and compassion. What can I do to help?"

Who is he? An angel or what? I couldn't believe my ears. Suddenly, all my questions and doubts about the invitation to Dr. Edward's lavish party were answered in one line from the senator. But why hadn't Dr. Edward mentioned Senator Ruth to us before? Maybe he didn't want us prepared. That would've made it look like some kind of ploy to get the senator in. If so, I had to admit it had worked—both Jessie and I were caught completely unprepared and surprised.

A butler had already served us whiskey, and as Jessie entered the room, he took her order and served her a glass of champagne. Jessie congratulated the senator for pushing through a controversial LGBT rights bill. She also told him about our goals and what we had achieved up to that point. Jessie had always been a popular girl; once again, her speech reminded me why. During her impromptu presentation, she hadn't forgotten to thank Dr. Edward. Jessie said, "We couldn't have done this without the help of Dr. Edward and his organization."

At that point, Dr. Edward seemed to feel compelled to say something. "Jessie, stop. It has all been possible because of you guys. The senator and I are here to help."

Senator Ruth agreed. "That's right, Jessie. Just tell us what you guys need."

I said, "We are now planning to conduct a few workshops for parents on the prevention of genetic diseases in all major US cities, and then at some point, we would like to push for mandatory carrier screening tests in the preconception period."

The senator said, "Although I cannot guarantee the outcome of the bill, I can try to push it through. We'll definitely need more senators on board. You can expect a loud opposition, too. Sometimes, we can only offer a solution, but we can't force people to accept it."

Jessie looked at the senator and said, "But polio and smallpox vaccination was once mandatory in the US and in many parts of the world. Why would this be any different?"

"I understand your frustrations, Jessie, but this is a very sensitive issue. Tell you what, you have my support, so let's do the first things first: let's spread the word and build a strong public opinion in the US." And he reached for his glass.

"Cigar?" asked Dr. Edward.

"Sure. Thank you, provided your guests here don't mind," said the senator with a smile.

I nodded, and Jessie said, "Please carry on. Don't mind us."

That was one afternoon in my life where I learned a lot of new things: what lavish parties really meant, how the rich did business, and how they could appear to be doing nothing and yet were on top of everything. The party was an eye-opener for me. Dr. Edward was so right: if we wanted to push for mandatory carrier screening tests, who would be a better person to approach than a senator?

Senator Ruth seemed sincere, and he was eager to help. He even told us to hold a workshop at his political strongholds in Connecticut. "My office can help," he said. "Just let me know when you guys are ready."

Chapter 12

Jessie and I left the party in the late afternoon to reach New York City by early evening. We had already promised to meet Susan and Kelly. They were both victims of the Iraq turmoil, having lost their husbands in the war. However, they had soon discovered they had more in common. Susan's daughter was diagnosed with Turner syndrome while Kelly's son had been suffering from cystic fibrosis for the last two years. Since joining the movement, they had made good progress in connecting many other parents of genetic disease victims in the greater New York City area.

Although we had never met face-to-face before, through regular phone calls and video chats, I felt like I had known them for a long time. Until we met Senator Ruth, I had always thought, with Susan and Kelly's help, New York City could be our base in the United States.

Kelly's house at Park Slope, Brooklyn, was close to two hours' drive from the Hamptons. Our trip to Dr. Edward's party had opened a new vista for the parental fitness test program in the US. The whole campaign could get a boost with the senator's help. But I also knew I couldn't have done it without Jessie's help. As our limo hit the NY 27 W/Southampton Bypass, I looked at her and said, "Thank you, Jessie."

"For what?" She turned her face from the falling sunlight coming through the window.

"You did a great job today. We had a good conversation with the senator. He sounds sincere."

"Yes, he does, but why are you thanking me? I was just doing my job," Jessie answered in a solemn voice.

Our conversations had become awkward ever since Dylan had reappeared in Jessie's life. We had hardly talked in the last few days. There was an uncanny distance. But I also knew it wouldn't go away until we both sat down and talked about it. A lot had happened since we had come back from Europe, and Dylan's coming back into the picture had further complicated our relationship. But instead of talking about it, I was practically running away from her. I asked myself, what was I afraid of? *The truth?*

There was no doubt we liked each other, but the odds were also stacked up high against us; we both had excess baggage. Maybe that's why we had never talked about any future. I was looking at an incurable disease, and my situation would only get worse from here after the onset.

But in spite of all that, Jessie had said on more than one occasion, "I'm happy now. I have never been happier." The truth was, I was happy, too, with our "one day at a time" routine. We used to look forward to our time together. However, all that had changed when Dylan came back. *I guess we didn't see that coming.*

But I had to get it all off my chest; maybe she needed that, too. The silence was driving me crazy. We should put everything out in the open and analyze what we were up against. But then again, I already knew Jessie's answer. She would do everything in her power to make her son happy, even if that meant sacrificing her own happiness. She had already told me that Lukas needed a father in his life. Besides, what could I offer?

I was sure this uneasy distance between us was also tearing her apart. That lively girl I knew in our high school, or even the one I had seen at the pub six months before had vanished, robbing Jessie of her usual warmth. She almost had stopped talking unless it became necessary. That's why, after her conversation with the senator, I thought for a moment that the old Jessie was back. Or as she said, was she just doing her job?

Jessie was still looking out the window. Her golden-yellow hair was shining against the falling sunlight. The side bangs almost fell down to her cheekbones. She made no efforts to flip them back, so I could see very little of her face. I would have loved to know what she was thinking about. We used to share everything until we came back from Europe. One month later, we didn't even know what to say to each other. And through the entire journey from the Hamptons to New York City, she didn't say another word.

Soon, the car pulled up in front of a nice two-story limestone house on Union Street. Since we weren't familiar with the New York City area, I had already handed over Kelly's address to the chauffeur. Thank god, Dr. Edward had arranged the car for us; otherwise, it would've been difficult to get back in time.

We were more than surprised as we entered the house. Susan and Kelly must have invited over twenty people to meet us. Most of them belonged to army families.

"Some people call us 'The NYC Army Wives,'" quipped one of them. Everyone laughed.

Thank god, Jessie knew what that lady was referring to. Jessie said, "I loved that show, although I didn't catch all the episodes." Then she looked at Kelly and said, "I'm a little over-dressed; may I use your bathroom?"

Jessie was right. We looked way formal for a house gathering. For those who didn't know our full itinerary, Kelly cleared up any confusion by saying, "You guys are coming straight from the party, right? How did that go?"

"Oh, it was great," said Jessie on her way out, "we made good progress this morning." Then she looked at me and asked, "David, why don't you start? I'll join you guys in a minute." And she left the room.

I quickly summed up our Parental Fitness Test Movement for our new friends. I also told them how a simple carrier screening test could put a stop to all these hereditary genetic diseases right away. The response from Europe surprised everyone, but our conversation with the senator that afternoon energized them the most.

"Isn't that great? Getting Senator Ruth on board is a big deal," said a guy in a wheelchair. An hour later, when I met Michael formally, he explained the wheelchair. He had lost both his legs in an explosion in Iraq, but he had no regrets, except that they couldn't find what they all went for—the much-talked-about WMD. And he laughed.

Michael and Molly had two sons, and the younger one suffered from galactosemia. Although Molly had been in touch with Susan and Kelly since they came on board, Michael never thought much about it.

"Another advocacy group? Please keep me out of it," had been his usual remark. But somehow, Molly had forced that evening on him. And when he heard about our meeting with Senator Ruth, he realized that we were darn serious. The senator's participation and approval meant a great deal to him. They were all Americans. They knew what Senator Ruth had done in the past, and to them, his support meant a lot. It took some time for me to realize the senator's power, but slowly, I was getting there.

Two days later, when I came home from New York City, I realized something: some people in our lives always stand by us like a lighthouse, silently guiding us to the shore. My mother was that lighthouse in my life. Since we had landed on a Sunday afternoon, I had missed a pre-arranged breakfast with my mother that morning. It wasn't the first time I had missed an appointment with my mother, but from the voicemail, this time, she sounded upset.

When I called her to apologize, she flared up. "Do you know I had already called you three times since this morning?" And before I could say anything in my defense, she continued. "You better come down now and have dinner here. I won't have time to see you until next Sunday. And we're already late."

"Late for what, Mom? What's so important that it can't wait until next Sunday? I promise I'll be there."

"No, it can't wait. Let me put it this way—we should've done it yesterday."

I didn't understand what she was talking about, but it seemed important to her, and I couldn't ignore that. I pulled out my jacket and decided to walk over.

When my mother opened the door, she looked baffled. Seeing my jacket covered in snowflakes, she removed the small door screen and peeped out. Not seeing my car in the driveway, she asked, "Why didn't you drive?"

"I wanted to walk back after dinner; I need the exercise since I missed my gym today."

"It's minus five degrees out there. Are you crazy or what?"

"It didn't quite feel that way," I tried to explain.

"Never mind. Get yourself a drink. Dinner will be ready in ten." And she went into the kitchen.

"Do you want one?" I shouted from the living room.

"You go ahead. I've got a glass of wine."

I had never been a regular drinker. I hesitated a couple of minutes in front of my mom's liquor cabinet—a small table with a few glasses and a couple of wine bottles. She also had a bottle of whiskey and a cognac. I deliberated for a minute, then poured myself a cognac and followed my mother into the kitchen. I was curious to know what all the fuss was about.

"Tell me now what is so important that it couldn't wait another week." I sat on the long end of the kitchen counter.

"I need you to sign some papers. Anyway, dinner is ready. Let's eat first."

Towards the end of the dinner, she suddenly asked, "How is your new girlfriend?"

"What do you mean by new girlfriend? Are you talking about Jessie?"

"Yes, your cheerleader friend," she clarified.

Given the latest series of complications, I would have hesitated to call Jessie my girlfriend anymore. In my book, girlfriends didn't have husbands. So, what was she? Recently, I had been asking myself that question every day.

"She isn't really my girlfriend."

"Why? What happened?" she asked.

"Let it go, Ma. It's complicated." I tried to put a stop to that conversation.

"Life is complicated, David. You have to press on," she said as she started clearing the table.

I got up and helped her clear the rest. I said, "I'm trying, Ma. I'll tell you everything as soon as I sort things out in my head. Let's sign those papers now."

She pulled out two thick piles of papers. I had seen those before. In fact, I had seen them all my life, and those piles used to be thicker. First, it was my dad's medical insurance file, and after my dad had passed away, my mother had created one for each of us.

"After your positive test for HD, I had to make changes in your policy. I need your signature." My mom pushed a thick, gray-colored file toward me.

"Why didn't you tell me? I could've had it done."

"Don't worry, it's already done. Just sign…" Her voice choked, so she got up and left the room in a hurry.

I remembered we had promised ourselves that we would never talk about my HD until the disease was actually upon us. But my mother had seen the disease closely for ten to twelve years, and she knew it would be silly not to be prepared this time. She knew even if I took care of myself through the early stages of the disease, I would need special care as the disease advanced. Everyone knew the middle and final stages of HD weren't pretty, and the patient would need 24/7 care. My mother was trying to put up a brave front, but her actions indicated, inside, she was panicking.

Needless to say, I was frightened, too. Ever since I got the confirmation, a day didn't go by when I didn't think about my plight in the near future. The constant fear had been eating me up. In my sleep or while I was awake, every time I saw a glimpse of my diseased future, I shivered and tried to push my thoughts away. But they came right back like a ping-pong ball.

To make sure I had not succumbed to the onset yet, I often tested my memory by trying to unwind the threads of random events from my life. I wanted to know I could still recall each incident thread by thread. I would panic if it took any longer than usual. *But what is the usual timeframe to recall old memories?* I had no idea, and I didn't really want to probe further.

But what was I afraid of? *Death is inevitable. It's our final destination as a mortal being. But death is never as scary as thoughts about it are. Besides, no one knows how long they have to suffer before death takes them away.* It could be a prolonged battle like my father had, or it could be quick. But HD was particularly terrifying because it would take away my physical and mental abilities one-by-one, robbing me of my normal daily activities. Paralyzed and unable to move, I would slowly become dependent on others. The thought alone numbed my senses. I didn't want to live like that.

But I hadn't discussed any of this with Jessie. I didn't want to drag her into my health problems. Whenever the thought came to mind, I would force myself to think of anything else but HD. But that had also caused a severe problem. By repressing the subject, I often woke up with a nightmare in the middle of a night.

One night, about a week ago, I had awoken with a scary thought: Jessie was kissing me, and in spite of my best efforts, I couldn't kiss her back. I had no senses in my tongue or on my lips—it felt dead cold. I had no saliva. My mouth was drying up fast. I desperately tried to feel something, but there was nothing. I only felt traumatized and numb inside. Tears rolled down my cheeks, and I woke up with a shock at the wet and cold feeling on my face.

My mother came back after ten minutes and asked, "You want apple pie?"

"Sure." I paused, looked her in the eye, and said, "Anyway, I have signed everything. And thank you for doing this, Mom."

"Don't worry about it. This was the least I could do."

"You've done plenty, Mom. I love you." I hugged her, and we both burst out crying. Uncontrollable tears rolled down our cheeks, robbing our voices. We stood there in the middle of our kitchen, our hands clutching each other. Intense and overwhelming sobs overtook us as, bit by bit, our thick façade came tumbling down. We held each other tight in our arms and kept on crying.

What had happened to our promises? What ignited the outburst? I didn't have a clue. But I realized one thing: a human touch is explosive. It's so warm that it melts away everything, including our ego. The moment we held each other, all other garbage, like intellectual reasoning, flew out the window. And we both admitted we were scared to death.

Chapter 13

In the middle of hopelessness and total chaos in my daily life since the blood test had confirmed my HD, the Carrier Screening Test campaign to prove parental fitness was the only thing that had given me a reason to wake up every morning. And I had to thank Jessie for that. Otherwise, waiting for death wasn't easy.

I had mentioned that to my counselor in our previous session last month: "That's the only thing I look forward to every day. Although this isn't the first career choice I had in mind, since we had started this project, I don't miss surgery that much. If I could get this bill approved, it would benefit millions of people. Hereditary genetic diseases would be a thing of the past."

Dr. Bergman wished me luck and asked me to be patient. She was right. The program would take time to gain momentum. But for me, the time was ticking, and God only knew how much time I had left.

Like in most offices, our Monday mornings were hectic. That week was especially so since both Jessie and I had been in New York City the last few days.

The events at my mom's place the previous night had also shaken me. I knew I was panicking inside as the days went by, but I hadn't had a clue that my mother had also been suppressing those tumultuous emotions. How much she must've had to suffer silently. I should have talked to her earlier.

I reached the office early, at about half-past eight, to get some work done before anyone else came in. I turned on my computer, and the emails came pouring in. *Two hundred and thirty-two unread emails?* I wished I had a cup of coffee. But we didn't have a coffeemaker yet, so instead of thinking about coffee, I tried to concentrate on my emails.

Minutes later, Jessie came in with two coffees in her hands. I didn't even greet her good morning; I shouted from my room, "Is that mine? You're a savior. But how did you know I was here?"

"Duh! I saw your car."

I thanked Jessie and said, "We're lucky to have a Tim Hortons downstairs."

And since Jessie was already in my room, I asked her whether she knew a Christina Hall. "She wants to meet us as soon as possible. I wonder why?"

"Did you ask Melissa?" asked Jessie.

"No, not yet. I saw the note this morning, stuck on my desk."

"Well, let's find out." She snatched the small Post-it note from my hand and walked out of the room.

I wanted her to stay. I had so many things I wanted to say to her. But I couldn't stop her; nothing came out of my mouth. I wasn't sure why my voice choked. What had happened? After all, we had become good friends in the last few months. I wanted to clear the air between us—tell her that, if she decided to get back with Dylan, she had my support. She had gone through a lot, and if Dylan could bring a smile to her face again, that would be great. But I also wanted to let her know about my feelings for her.

With last night's emotional outbursts, I had also gotten another reality check: everyone around me must be feeling nervous, but they weren't saying anything.

Like any sensible person, I wanted to be prepared for my final days. *But how does one do that?* It wasn't like preparing for a marathon or a final exam. Everyone knew HD was a slow and painful process. But that wasn't the worst—the hideous part was it could start as early as the next day or maybe ten years later. No one could predict an onset of the disease.

But why was I thinking like I was dying? The depressing thoughts set off by those insurance papers the previous night were pulling me down. *Perhaps a walk outside would help.* I wanted to clear my head, and I refused to succumb to fear. *The disease is one thing; that's a reality, but the fear isn't. What am I doing?* I had been staring at the computer screen for an hour and hadn't read a single email. I stormed out of my room and walked to the main door.

"David, wait up." I heard Jessie's voice as I passed by her room.

I took a few steps back and asked, "What's up?"

"Where are you going?"

"To take a walk."

"Now? Is everything okay with you?" Jessie couldn't suppress her concern.

"Everything is fine, Jessie. Tell me, what is it?"

"I spoke with Christina. She said she—"

But I interrupted her. "Who is Christina?"

"Remember, the note you gave me this morning? Christina Hall?" Jessie explained.

"Oh, I'm sorry. What did she say?"

"You know where she lives? Right here, at Brentwood. She wants to meet us right away. I am driving there a little later. You want to go?"

"I have tons of work here. You go ahead."

But Jessie said, "Aren't you going for a walk anyway? So, spending some time out of the office might help you clear your head. Come on, what do you say?"

It suddenly occurred to me that driving with Jessie might give me some time to talk outside our office, and I agreed.

We left for Christina's place by about ten-thirty in the morning, and after driving for a while, I suddenly said, "I love you, Jessie."

"I love you, too," expressed Jessie promptly, and she held my hand.

"But —" I tried to tell her about Dylan.

However, Jessie interrupted and said, "Whoa, whoa, whoa! Wait a minute, you mean that comes with a 'but'?"

"Can you please let me finish first? What I mean is, if you want to get back with Dylan, I support that, too."

"In the first place, why would you think that?"

I wanted to explain, but we had already reached Brentwood. It was only a fifteen-minute drive. Jessie said she was still sorting out stuff with Dylan, and we decided to continue the conversation later.

A beautiful two-story house in a quiet, upscale neighborhood in Calgary stood before us. Christina welcomed us with freshly brewed coffee. "I baked some cookies last night. James loves them," Christina said. "Want to try some?"

"I don't mind a taste." Jessie followed Christina to the kitchen.

They both came back with a plate full of cookies to add to the pile of muffins that Christina had already put in the dining room.

When Christina finally sat down on a chair in front of me, I asked, "How did you find us?"

"My cousin, Robert, told me about you guys. He was all praises about both of you. He said that, if not for anything else, I should call you guys for a chat to get a fresh perspective on the disease."

"Does he know us?" I asked. "I'm sure we'd love to meet him, too."

"You guys have already met him," answered Christina.

"We did?" Jessie blurted out with cookies in her mouth. We both looked at each other and tried to recall any Robert we had met recently.

Realizing our confusion, Christina said, "Think Senator Ruth—Robert Ruth?"

"Oh my god, you're Senator Ruth's cousin?"

And at that moment, I was able to put one unsolved puzzle together. At Dr. Edward's party, while we were walking back from the helipad to the library, he had mentioned something about the senator's nephew suffering from HD. He also had said that's what prompted the senator to take an active role in our movement. I wondered how that information got buried in my memory. I had no recollection of that until Christina mentioned it again. I had never had such a memory lapse in the past. Never. *Could this be the beginning of the end for me?*

I came back to my senses as Jessie kicked me with her left leg from under the table. Christina told us that she had married young and moved to Calgary with her husband, Bruce. Two and a half years later, her husband had left town with a girl, half his age, and he had never come back. Christina had felt too sad and humiliated to go look for him. She had filed a missing person's report the next day and then picked up the pieces. The mother-and-son family was doing just fine until James was diagnosed with HD about four years ago. And as she reached that part of her story, her voice cracked, and her eyes filled with tears. "I'm sorry," mumbled Christina.

Jessie got up and pulled her chair closer to Christina and held her hand. We were all quiet for a while. Throughout the morning, I had been thinking I was the most unlucky guy in the whole world, but after hearing Christina's story, I wouldn't dare imagine what she must have gone through. Life had taken away everything from her. *First, her husband and now, her son? How cruel was that?* I thought of another person who was facing exactly the same reality. I said, "You have a lot in common with my mother."

"How so?" Christina couldn't suppress her curiosity.

"For one, my dad died of HD about twelve years ago, and I have HD too."

Christina almost flipped from her chair. "What are you talking about? You have HD?"

"Yes, the genetic test came back positive about a year ago."

"That must be hard on your mother. How does she cope with all that? More importantly, how does she look at your career choice?"

"I guess, like any other mother, she is also scared to death. That said, she is a very strong lady, and she somehow manages to work through her stress. But don't get me started on what she has to say about my career choices."

"Does she look at it as a condemnation against her and her husband, your father, to where they shouldn't have had you in the first place?"

"No, god no. Nothing of that sort. Yes, when she first heard I had HD, she blamed herself. But she totally loves this program. My mother said she would have been the first one to sign up had their OB told her about a carrier screening test back then. But she is mad at me because I didn't accept the heart surgeon's job at the Christchurch hospital."

"You mean you're a doctor, too?"

"Oh, that's just a paper qualification now. I don't practice medicine anymore."

Christina looked me in the eye and said, "What you're doing now is much bigger. I'm sure this will benefit many."

"I hope so. I hope, someday, I can make my mother proud again with that."

"You will. And since you're a qualified doctor, may I ask you a question? Something has been bugging me for the last couple of years."

"What is it?" I asked Christina.

"Well, I also keep blaming myself for James's condition. I wonder why my OB never said anything about any carrier screening test, although he asked us whether we had any genetic diseases in our family history. Maybe things would have been different. But tell me one thing: could we have taken any precautionary measures like gene alteration if we had found an affected gene in either of us?"

"Yes, you could've done that. But it's still not legal in Canada, the US, and many other developed countries. Once approved, for couples who have one partner affected with any single-gene diseases, In Vitro Fertilization with Prenatal Genetic Diagnosis is the only way available to make sure their kids don't inherit the affected genes. But the problem is, in most cases, parents don't even know they have any genetic disorders. By the time they realize it in their late thirties or early forties, it's too late; they may already have kids. And that's why we are recommending a carrier screening test for all parents. After that, the parents can sit down and decide a course of action."

"I realize the need for carrier screening tests, and I think that's going to be a game-changer, but I still don't understand gene editing clearly," said Christina.

Jessie came to my rescue. "Frankly, I also didn't get it at first. IVF with PGD is a procedure to make sure the implanted embryo is free of any genetic disorders. It tests the embryos for affected genes first before any implantation is made to create a pregnancy."

"I see," Christina paused for a while. "Thank you, guys. I wish I had known we had this problem. Like David said, by the time I found out James had HD, it was already too late. Maybe that's why Robert is pushing for this Carrier Screening Test."

"Exactly," said Jessie.

"Well, let's go see James now." Christina got up from her chair.

As we approached James's room, we could hear the loud sound of video games from the hallway. "Sorry about that," Christina apologized.

"Don't worry, my son does that all the time," Jessie replied.

"I didn't know you had a son. How old is he?"

"He's five. He suffers from hemophilia," said Jessie with her eyes on Christina.

"I'm sorry. How is he doing?"

"Oh, he's okay now. He goes to regular elementary school next year, and I'm scared to death."

"Don't worry, everything will be okay," assured Christina.

As soon as we stepped into James's room, his friend, Arthur, jumped out of the bed and said, "Bye, Bro, I'll come back later."

"No, not so fast, dear," Christina said. "Didn't I tell you to sit on a chair and not on his bed?"

"I'm sorry, ma'am. It won't happen again." He dodged us and got out of the room.

"What are you afraid of, Mom? There's no bigger germ that can kill me any faster," quipped James.

At first glance, James looked like any sixteen-year-old boy, but his movements had already become seriously impaired. He couldn't do much without help anymore. The day-nurse, Annabelle—a young woman in her early twenties—was sitting at one corner when we came in, but she left the room as we pulled our chairs close to James.

"When was the first time you suspected HD or something different?" I asked James.

"About four years ago," answered Christina.

"That's a lie, Mom, and you know that." He turned his face toward me and said, "Five years ago, for nearly one year, every time I said something was wrong, both my mother and the doctor ignored it, and they always treated me for something I didn't have."

"Did your father have HD?"

"You see, that's the thing, no one knows. My father is MIA. He left us a long time ago, and my mother here has no clue what he had or didn't have."

"Stop. Stop. What's the point now?" cried Christina.

"Why, Mom?" James again looked me in the eye and said, "I don't know who you guys are and why you're here, but if you're here to help us, help my mother. She needs it; you can't help me.

"Anna," James called out, and Annabelle appeared within seconds. "I want to turn." And she helped him turn to the other side, away from us.

We also turned back. And all the time we were in that room, Jessie hadn't said a word. Why? Did Christina's situation with her husband, leaving behind their sick son, remind Jessie of Dylan?

Jessie finally opened her mouth on the landing. "Maybe we shouldn't have bothered him. Looks like he isn't in a good mood today."

Christina sighed. "That seldom happens these days."

"Don't worry. The idea here is to see how you two are coping with the disease. We're here for both of you," Jessie explained to Christina.

Christina described how they had all misunderstood James's problems at first. "We were so stupid. We never thought of HD in our wildest dreams because we didn't know anyone had HD in the family."

"What about his father's side of the family?" I asked.

"That's another thing. I never knew much about his father's family. They are from Pennsylvania. We visited them once after James was born, and that's it. Bruce never talked about them, and once he left us, it was like their whole family had gone off the radar."

"It must've been tough." Jessie extended her left hand to hold Christina's.

"You've no idea," sighed Christina.

"I can imagine. I've been through the same," said Jessie. "We're practically sisters." She leaned toward Christina, and they hugged each other.

"When did you first diagnose him with HD?" I asked.

"As I said, we didn't think of HD until about four years ago. When he turned eleven, he started losing his concentration and became more forgetful. At first, I thought little of it. I presumed it was a typical adolescent problem. You know how kids are these days.

"But his teacher pointed out something. She said, 'James is a good student. He's attentive in class, and he fares well in his in-class tests, but he can't answer the same questions on a test later.'

"That got me worried. He had his whole life ahead of him, but the doctors had found nothing wrong. They treated him for attention deficit, but with no positive development. Six to seven months later, I noticed his memory lapses at home, too. And then, he developed twitches here and there. I got scared, and I rushed to the doctor again. The doctor said it could be Transient Tics, common with ADHD patients, and that it should go away on its own. Although they would test him for Tourette's syndrome after one year if that didn't subside."

"Did that go away on its own?" asked Jessie.

"No, it didn't. But I couldn't wait for another year for them to diagnose him. His condition was deteriorating even further. He severely lacked coordination, and his movements became jerky. One of my colleagues told me to take him to a neurologist. And that was the first time the clinic diagnosed him with HD. I had no idea what I was dealing with."

"Oh my god! That must've been some experience," cried Jessie.

"And that was just the beginning," said Christina as she got up from her chair at the sound of an alarm bell. "Sorry about the alarm; I try to maintain a fixed time for his lunch and dinner." She paused and then looked at Jessie and me and said, "Have lunch with me, and I promise we'll talk about something else."

"Sorry, we have to do lunch another day. I'm bit tied up today. Maybe we can come back next week?" Jessie said.

"Sure. I know how busy you guys are; Robert told me all about that. But I won't take any excuse the next time."

Jessie went to visit the loo before leaving, and I got up from the sofa, said goodbye to Christina, and headed for the front porch to wait there.

The neighborhood looked quiet and peaceful. The long street was empty with no one in sight. I had parked my car on the main street, and dry leaves were already covering it. But every time I wanted to think of something else, James's face appeared before me, desperately clinging on. I sat down on a long bench in one corner. I shivered, thinking what that little guy must have been going through. I had seen my father suffering through those stages, but I was a kid back then. Most things made little sense at that time. I also realized, in the coming years, the same would happen to me as well.

After we got in the car, we were both speechless for a while. I said, "To think of it, that's me in the near future. The only unknown part is how near. It can start in a few months or in a few years. Do you really want all that in your life?"

"I'm willing to take that gamble. Trust me, I have no illusions about love. Love has nothing to do with how long you live with a person," Jessie said. "It's about the emotional intensity that dictates your life while living with that person. One good kiss can last a lifetime in your memory."

I understood what she meant. *But after everything Jessie has gone through in her life, she deserves happiness now. Can I make her happy? How could she be happy with a person who is treading at the threshold of an HD onset?*

That night, after a long time, I woke up again soon after I went to sleep. I still didn't know how to define or describe that uncanny feeling. I wasn't sleeping for sure, but I wasn't awake either, as I had no control over my physical movements. It was deeper than deep-thinking.

In a bizarre, cryptic dream, I found myself lying in James's bed with Annabelle attending to me. But I couldn't get my head around why my family had put me there. We hardly knew them. *Where is Jessie? Where is my mother? This is ridiculous.* I was reeling from the new setting. *Well, if I am in James's bed, where is he? Is he dead already?* I shivered even thinking it.

"Aww!" I heard someone mocking me. And there he was, at one corner, laughing and sitting on a window sill.

"This isn't funny. What are you smiling about?" I asked.

"You know what, I didn't tell you everything," said James.

"Well, you can tell me now." I looked at him eagerly.

"On one condition—you can't tell anyone."

"Okay, okay."

"You promise?"

"Yes, I promise."

"Nope, that won't do. Spit shake?" He spat on his right palm and held it toward me.

Although I didn't like it, I had no choice, and I obliged him. I wanted to know more about what he was going through. I wanted to be ready for my turn. So I did as he had asked. But the moment my hand touched his palm to shake hands, I got an electric shock from him. "What's that?"

"Exactly. That's what I wanted to tell you. I can buzz any-body now."

"What do you mean?"

"I have this feeling of electric current moving through my body the whole day. Did you like it?"

"No, I didn't. This isn't funny. This is painful."

The sudden shock felt like I had just been electrocuted. The pain was excruciating. I curled up and pressed my right hand with the left palm to avoid the throbbing.

The pain felt so real that I woke up with a shock again, feeling sweaty and sticky. I threw away the comforter.

I turned on the light and got up from the bed. My throat was all dried up, and I walked to the kitchen to get a glass of water. Seeing James earlier that day from such close proximity was like seeing myself in the mirror—only a couple of years' ahead of time.

Chapter 14

The next morning, I woke up with a severe headache, still thinking about my uncanny dream. Since my dad had passed away, I hadn't seen HD so close. James's condition had shaken me badly.

I knew James hadn't told me anything about the feeling of electric current moving through his body. I had read that in a magazine a few months ago, and obviously, the previous night, I had been hallucinating again. Still, I wanted to see him. *But why?* Why did I suddenly feel so close to him? Just because we were suffering from the same disease? Or did I see my future in him? I didn't have the answer, but that didn't matter. I told myself that spending some time with a dying sixteen-year-old kid couldn't be a bad idea.

I wanted to know what was going on in his head. So, instead of driving to the office, I went straight to Christina's house again. But as soon as I parked the car opposite their house, I froze, thinking my sudden visit might look kind of odd. I should've called first. I couldn't just drop by. But I also didn't have Christina's number on me, so I texted Jessie for the number.

Christina was warm and welcoming on the phone. She said, "Please don't hesitate. Drop by anytime you want. And I'm sure James will like that, too."

Five minutes later, I knocked on Christina's door. After a little chit-chat and a cup of coffee, I headed for James's room. James was lying on his back with his eyes closed, listening to his music, or at least, it looked that way. Annabelle had covered him with a white sheet up to his chest. It was a scary sight: a six-teen-year-old boy fighting for his life—or maybe, not fighting and waiting to die. He knew his condition wouldn't improve, and there was no cure for his illness. To be more accurate, he was well aware that his condition would only deteriorate from there, and all he could hope for in the coming days was more pain and more suffering. *How does one cope with that?* I was hoping to get some answers from him.

James opened his eyes as Annabelle told him he had a visitor. He looked at me from one corner of his eyes and said, "It's you again. Where's your girlfriend? … You want to listen?" He offered me one of the earplugs and said, "Rascal Flatts."

"Oh, I love them too. But now, I would rather talk."

"Talk about what? What's there to talk?"

"I understand your frustration. I also have HD."

"So? Does that make you my pal and qualified to read my mind?"

"Nope. In fact, none of that. But I saw my father suffering and going through the same thing."

"Well, that's good for you, but no one told me anything about any of this. I didn't know my father had HD. And I don't care about that now. I was going about doing my regular business—school, games, and hanging out with my buddies—the regular stuff, you know. Then, one day, kaboom! I found out I had HD." James paused. He showed me the water cup on the table with his eyes. I brought the cup close to his mouth. He took one sip with the straw attached to the cup and closed his eyes.

"You know what, they all used to come every day to see me—John, Sofia, Lulu, Richard, and Nick—that Korean guy, too. But now they all disappeared. I get it, they're busy. If I were in school, I'd be busy, too," James said in one breath, and he paused again. At this stage, it looked like he didn't have the strength to continue. He looked exhausted, and he closed his eyes.

Annabelle had been keeping a close watch on us from the next room. She walked over to James and said, "I think you have said enough for now. We need to prepare for your bath. But first, you rest for ten minutes." Then, she looked at me and said, "Christina is waiting for you downstairs. Please give us half an hour. I apologize for the interruption."

That was clearly my cue to leave, but I wasn't done yet. He was just opening up, and I wanted to know more. So I went downstairs to hang with Christina until James had finished his bath.

"Did you talk to him? He doesn't speak much these days. Who would believe just five to six years ago, he was one of the smartest guys in his school? His friends used to call him 'the cool dude,' and look at him now," Christina lamented.

"He's still the cool dude, Christina. He just chooses not to speak much. This transition isn't easy and especially for a boy of his age."

"I know. I wish I could do something. I feel so helpless."

"We all feel the same way, Christina. Genetic disease in any family is bad news."

A sudden phone call from Jessie made me realize that I hadn't even informed her about my whereabouts that morning. Her voice seemed worried, though she said nothing about it. I told her I had wanted to settle something in this part of the town and I had dropped by at Christina's place.

"What something?" she asked.

I wasn't prepared for that question. "Nothing important. I'll explain when I reach the office." To lighten the situation, I said, "Christina makes very nice coffee. You want to join us?"

"No, David, I don't. I'll see you when I see you." And she hung up.

Christina realized from my face that it didn't go well. She said, "I think she's worried about you."

"I know. Well, let me finish with James and get going." I headed back upstairs again.

Christina stood up, handed me my half-finished coffee, and said, "Why don't you take it with you?"

James was already lying on his bed, and he must have said something funny because Annabelle was still laughing, sitting by his bedside. As I knocked on the open door, she rose to her feet, her face looking flushed. Annabelle was a few years older than James, and she connected well with him—and it was obvious that she cared for him more than just as a patient. She looked at James and asked, "Do you want to sit up?"

"Sure," said James.

Annabelle rolled up the bed. She still had that smile at the corner of her lips. She took a quick glance at James and left the room.

I spoke with James that day for another hour until his lunch time. He told me a lot of things from his schooldays and about his old friends. "But that's all gone. Now, I have only one friend—Anna."

"How about Arthur? Isn't he a friend too?" I asked.

"I guess so. But I don't like to play video games anymore. A year ago, I used to beat him every time we played, but now I can't keep up."

"You guys can do other things too, right?"

"Like what? If we didn't play video games, he wouldn't come," James said.

But we were interrupted as Annabelle entered the room with his lunch.

I said, "We'll catch up another day. Enjoy your lunch."

Although Christina wanted me to have lunch with her, I didn't want to keep Jessie waiting. I excused myself and headed for the office.

Every email we got from a genetic disease victim or from their families was a stark reminder that we were running against time. Spreading the awareness to sign up for a Carrier Screening Test before having a child was the only answer to our problems. In the last month, we had focused our resources on organizing the first workshop in our hometown, Calgary. When the day finally came, I confronted something I'd never experienced before: an auditorium full of people eager to hear what we had to say. God knew I had never been a public speaker. All I could show for myself in that particular arena were a few paper presentations in our medical school. Although we had been waiting for the workshop for such a long time, when the stage was set, I felt very nervous.

There were six chairs for the panelists on the stage, two for the guests, and one for the host of the show. And the host was none other than our dear Jessie. She was a born natural at all this. She knew how to engage people. As she went on stage, she welcomed everyone and set the ground rules for the discussion to proceed. She also engaged a few volunteers to pass around the microphones during the Q&A session. She introduced the speakers and said, "This isn't a convention or a seminar. This is just a discussion platform. It's not much about etiquette, but we need to maintain basic discipline. Otherwise, we won't get anything done. So, let's get the discussions started."

Having the first workshop in our hometown was Jessie's idea. She said, "This will help us get a feel of what's coming. In case there's a hiccup, people here will be more forgiving of us."

I couldn't agree more. Besides, I knew I could always rope in Dr. Tyler if we did the workshop in Calgary. He was a great speaker. I could pick up a few pointers from him; he had all sorts of experiences. And on that day, he gave an excellent opening speech with a brief yet thorough overview of the genetic diseases as we knew them. Thank god, Jessie had arranged to videotape the whole event because, that day onward, I would probably be the one delivering that speech. And that recording would be helpful for our overseas volunteers, too.

A month later, we had our second workshop at the Hartford Community Hall. We were new in Connecticut, but the senator's team had facilitated everything, and we were told to be there just one day before the event. After all, it was his town. We also got Susan and Kelly to mobilize their contacts from New York City.

To be frank, none of us had expected any big crowd at Hartford. We would've been perfectly happy with even fifty to sixty people for our first workshop in the US. But the turnout surprised us all. The auditorium was full to the brim. Later we were told it had a capacity to hold three hundred people.

Like we did the first time, Jessie went to the microphone to introduce the speakers. The first fifteen minutes of my presentation also went on smoothly—there was pin-drop silence in the auditorium. Those who came had a personal interest in the program. They were either a friend or family of a victim. They all wanted to find solutions to their problems. Everyone was listening attentively until one gentleman in the third row got up and started voicing his concerns.

I wasn't a veteran speaker. I didn't know how to handle a sudden disruption. He stood up and asked, "Who are you to question a parent's fitness? What about our freedom of choice? You just can't force your ideas on us. Have you exhausted all other options? What about gene editing?"

"Please let me finish first, sir, and I will answer all your questions." I tried to calm him down.

"Why don't you answer the questions first, and if we feel satisfied, we'll listen to your jibber-jabber later?" answered the gentleman.

The fact was, I wasn't ready for a Q&A until much later. I would've loved to answer all his queries, but his abrupt questions threw me off my game. The gentleman must've realized my weakness and started chanting, "Answer first…answer first."

Soon, two suited security guys appeared from the back and tried to calm him down. But failing to bring the situation under control, they wanted to escort him out. I felt helpless. That certainly hadn't gone well. I tried to draw their attention. "Excuse me, sir."

But no one listened. Then Jessie jumped up and came to the microphone. "Hello? Leave that gentleman alone." She was trying to grab the attention of the security guys, but maybe they weren't tuned to listening to anyone but their commander. And unfortunately, the senator hadn't been able to attend the workshop due to a family emergency—he'd already apologized for that. In any case, the security guards ignored Jessie at first, but she was persistent. "I'm calling the senator now." And she waved her cell phone.

The two suited guys guarding that gentleman immediately turned around and stood still. This time, Jessie addressed them directly. "Listen, this is a workshop, not a conference or seminar on genetic diseases. This is a platform for people to discuss a way out of a serious problem. Sure, we need discipline to carry this thing forward, but you also have to understand that people here are victims of deadly diseases. They're either the victims or friends and family of victims, so, chances are, everyone is emotionally charged in here. If anything goes wrong, blame it on the disease, and not on any person."

Abruptly, the whole auditorium burst out clapping. Everybody stood up and applauded Jessie's humane and sincere appeal. She raised her hands to calm them down, then she thanked them and asked them to take their seats. She turned her head to the backstage guys waiting at the side and said, "May I request another chair on the dais?" Then, she looked to the audience and said, "Now, I would like to invite our speaker from the audience to share his views. Come on up, sir."

Another round of applause followed. But the gentleman refused to move. He said, "That won't be necessary. I'll be quiet."

"Why not? You raised an important question."

"I did?"

"Of course, sir. We're very hopeful about gene editing. This is the closest we've ever got in fighting any lethal genetic disorders, like cystic fibrosis, thalassemia, HD, and some forms of Alzheimer's disease. But gene editing is still not available to all. If we are lucky, maybe our children's children will be able to take advantage of that. But a carrier screening test can stop the menace right now. It's up to you, and not dependent on further FDA approval. It's already approved."

Needless to say, the gentleman came up on stage and sat with us for the rest of the program, and from then on, it went smoothly—though it did result in an impromptu discussion on gene editing.

One of our panelists, Dr. Gregory Duncan, said, "We need to see this gene-editing development in the light of what is already available now. At present, the only way one can prevent genetic disease is by using IVF and Pre-implementation Genetic Diagnosis. With IVF and PGD combined, prospective parents can always create several embryos to choose before insemination."

"Editing the DNA of a human embryo to prevent a genetic disease in a baby is possible, but still not legally available in many countries, including in the US. So why don't we welcome taking a carrier screening test for the interim period?" asked Dr. Patricia Holden.

I said, "There's an even bigger problem on the ground. In most cases, young parents don't think that they are carrying genetic diseases. When the symptoms appear and they're finally diagnosed in their late thirties or early forties, they may already have kids. Or they could just be carriers, and then, it's too late. People don't usually go looking for a solution unless they see a problem. Whereas a simple carrier screening test can easily check if either parent has any genetic disorder. And only then they can think of possible solutions. Carrier screening tests do not become redundant once gene editing is approved. In fact, the tests complement the remedy."

The disruptions at the Hartford workshop weren't half as bad as I had feared. The next morning, Jessie showed me a few news reports in the local dailies. One paper headlined: "Want to be a parent? Take a fitness test." Another showed Jessie on the microphone and read, "Gene editing is too far away; Parental Fitness Test is here."

"Do I look fat here?" asked Jessie.

"Look again." I pushed the paper toward her. "Are you kidding me? You look great. The senator must have influenced the media to have such coverage."

"No, David, you've done it. Give yourself some credit. Of course, the senator's help made it all possible, I don't deny that."

"Well, we did it. I couldn't have done it without you. See, whose picture is plastered on all the newspapers?" I opened the papers one more time.

"Yeah, how about that? Finally, people are recognizing my hidden talents." She smiled.

I hadn't seen her smile like that for a long time. Since we had come back from Europe, there was always something or the other coming in-between our relationship. First, it was Dylan and then the workshops. The one in Calgary was rather easy, but we had been very stressed about the workshop at Hartford. After all, this was our first in the US, and we knew the future of the bill would depend a lot on that performance. But what we didn't know was that Senator Ruth was a media darling and his pet projects always got huge media attention.

Still, that day, I wasn't thinking about any of that; I was just glad to see a smile again on Jessie's face. I knew from the beginning that our relationship would be a challenge. Jessie always blamed herself for her son's illness. In fact, that was the sole reason for her involvement in our movement. She would do anything for her son's happiness, even if that came at the cost of our relationship. *But can we really have a lasting relationship? With my HD staring me in the eye, can I even make her happy?*

Chapter 15

When we become weak or face major dilemmas in life, we often look to God or to the universe to guide us by telling us what to do or by giving us some kind of a signal. Sometimes, we can plan all we want, but there seems to be a master planner who does exactly what he wants. I had already had some experiences of that in the past. I had always thought I would be a heart surgeon, but I guess someone had other plans for me.

And then, just when Jessie and I had resumed talking normally, Dylan showed up again—this time, with a proposal to take Jessie and Lukas back to London. He claimed his father had finally accepted Jessie as his wife and Lukas as their grandson, but I couldn't figure out why, after four years of absence, Dylan had suddenly shown up three times in the last three months. *Was that a sign from the universe? Would Jessie and Lukas really be better off in London with Dylan?*

An interesting email from Jason in Sydney brought me back to my work. First, he complimented us on our recent successes. Our workshops had worked miracles for us in Canada. The voluntary signatures had shot up to close to nine hundred thousand worldwide.

"Come to Sydney and let's make it a million within this month," wrote Jason in the email. I had already delayed a trip to Australia and New Zealand for a long time. My trip might also give Jessie some space to talk to Dylan freely. Besides, Jessie and I were trying to cover more ground by taking individual assignments.

The following week, I packed my bags and embarked on a whirlwind tour. I wanted to cover Sydney, Auckland, Singapore, Malaysia and Bangkok in ten days. I didn't know whether I was running to something or running away from facing the truth of losing Jessie forever. Of course, I wanted all OB/GYN providers to offer carrier screening tests to all parents in the preconception period, and I was ready to do anything to make that a reality. But I was also suffering from a major dilemma and an excruciating pain inside. For the last ten to eleven months, I had prepared myself for all kinds of physical pains associated with HD. I knew the day was coming. But what I couldn't bear was the thought of losing Jessie. Dylan's sudden reappearance from Jessie's past took me totally off-guard.

When Jessie and I had met again, six or seven months before, we weren't sure what we wanted. We both had baggage and were tired. We found a mutual connection in our pain and suffering. We embraced each other and held on tight. We had no idea where we were going with that, but we also had no expectations. We had never thought it would lead to anything. But it did.

However, now that Dylan has come back, perhaps I should step aside. If I loved Jessie, I had to see things from her point of view. I had to admit this was the first time in a long time Dylan had come up with something tangible for Jessie to consider. And Dylan was Lukas's father. Over time, they would bond just fine. Dylan had been pressing Jessie for an answer, and I wanted to leave that decision to Jessie. She already knew how I felt about her. But she should also know that she had my blessing if she decided to go to London with Lukas and Dylan. I had tried to tell her that on the day we met Christina and James, but she had refused to listen, cutting the conversation short before I could finish. Also, Dylan's new proposal hadn't existed at that point. *So, I must tell her again what I'd wanted to say, as early as possible.*

Once I got to Australia, work swept me away. We got massive responses in Sydney. Auckland was good, too. Jason was right: signatures for voluntary carrier screening tests were pouring in by the day, and Jason was closing in on his magic million by the end of the month.

In comparison, Southeast Asia was lukewarm. I knew it wouldn't be easy there—the people living in those countries had already warned me. But I was thinking about those few who could think past their barricades. They didn't care about the odds. Why should I? I wanted to be there for those who had already been fighting an uphill task. Proposing something like a compulsory carrier screening test in any country was tough, but I wanted to motivate them. I simply told them what I had been telling myself every day: "Even if just one couple takes a carrier screening test, that's a solid win for us. That's one step closer to our dream. After that, I will simply work hard to add one more, then one more, and then one more, until I have my last breath."

I flew back to Calgary on Saturday night. It was a bit of a rush all right, but I was desperate to catch Jessie on Sunday. I had to talk to her as soon as possible.

"Good morning. Did I catch you at a bad time?" I called Jessie the next morning.

"What time is it there? Where are you now?" asked Jessie.

"I'm at home. Did I wake you up?"

"Not at all. When did you come back? I wasn't expecting you until tomorrow." Jessie sounded surprised and happy, too.

"I was lucky to get a faster connection."

"What time did you reach home? Why didn't you call me to pick you up from the airport?"

"Nah, I didn't want to bother you. I reached here late last night."

"How is that a bother? Sometimes, you're weird."

"Let's talk about that another day. Now, are you free for lunch today?"

"Sure, I'm free."

"It's settled then. I'll pick you up at half past twelve." I hung up and walked up and down the length of my living room. Although I had rehearsed my lines throughout the trip, I didn't know what Jessie would say in response.

I took Jessie to a Spanish restaurant. She loved Spanish food. She kissed me and asked, "What's all this for?"

"No occasion. I have some stuff to discuss with you."

"Oh goodie, I have news too." Jessie giggled.

"Well, you go first," I said. I wanted to get everything out of the way.

"That wouldn't be fair, right? But who cares?" Her eyes sparkled.

"Go ahead." I was getting curious. What could it be? We had spoken almost every day on the phone, but she hadn't mentioned anything.

"Dylan is out of my hair for six months. He left town yesterday. His office called him back to put him in their Ho Chi Minh office to oversee a new project," she declared. "He can't come back here until that project takes off, which could take up to six months. I'm always worried when Lukas is with him. I know this joint custody thing won't work. If necessary, I'll fight him in court when he comes back."

"But didn't he ask you guys to move to London with him?"

"Yes, he did. But frankly, I don't know how Lukas feels about that. He loves to spend time with his dad, but he also complains when Dylan leaves. Besides, does Lukas want to leave everything here and move to London? I think it's a big question mark. I need time to understand what he wants and needs."

I had nothing to say to that. At that point in time, I was more concerned with the immediate task I had on hand. Should I deliver my speech as I had practiced it for the last few days, or should I hold on until it became necessary? *If Dylan is out of the picture for the next six months, my speech can wait. Even if she doesn't love Dylan, Jessie might sacrifice her love for Lukas's happiness. But what about her happiness? Besides, she still doesn't know what Lukas wants.* But my speech would break her heart. *So why do it now?*

The unexpected bonus of Dylan being gone for the next six months sounded like a windfall, yet I found myself wondering if I was stealing Jessie from Dylan by enjoying her company in the meantime. But I couldn't resist the temptation of spending the next six months with her again, uninterrupted. I was sure the universe had a way of working things out. *My speech can change nothing for the next few months, so what's the rush? Maybe I can find a way to make this transition easier for Jessie.*

I looked out the window and saw nothing but the empty street outside. The rows of maple trees covered in snow on both sides of the road reminded me of the subtle changes in life. It was almost the end of spring, although it felt more like winter in Calgary. *Who knows what's going to happen this summer or in early autumn?* Six months was a long time for a man who had an undated death sentence hanging over his head.

Jessie looked me in the eye and said, "Anyway, forget Dylan. Tell me what you wanted to discuss."

But at that point in time, after what Jessie had told me, I didn't want to discuss anything. I just wanted to look at her face. I wished time stood still. I said, "On second thought, it's nothing that can't wait. Let's enjoy our time together now and keep that discussion for tomorrow. What do you say?"

"I like that very much," she said with a smile. She looked happy.

But the next morning, as I met Jessie in the office, she asked, "What's that important stuff you wanted to discuss yesterday?"

"What important stuff?"

"You said we'd talk about it today." She tried to jog my memory.

"I can't remember. I'm drawing a blank."

"No worries. Possibly it's not important. Tell me when it comes back to you. Anyway, how are you feeling?"

"I'm feeling great, but why do you ask?"

"No reason. Catch you later." She disappeared into her own room.

After more than a week out of the office, I had a lot to catch up on, and I dove in. Almost an hour later, one email from Jessie addressed to Kelly jogged my memory. Unknowingly, she must have copied me on the email. She wrote that she thought I had been avoiding her, and she had no idea "why."

In the last few months, she had become quite close with Kelly and Susan, and perhaps she had told them more about us than they needed to know. The email reminded me that I hadn't told her yet why I had asked her out for lunch the previous day. My much-rehearsed speech had become useless once I'd heard Jessie's side of the story, but I had to come clean. However, before I could think of a time and place to talk about that, Jessie pushed open the door. "Hey, got a minute?"

"Sure, what's up?"

"Do you remember the date of our workshop in Calgary?" Jessie asked.

"Hang on a minute." I opened the file on my computer and gave her the date. But instead of leaving, she pulled up a chair and sat down.

"Do you have the dates of your Auckland and Sydney workshops?"

"Sydney on the fifth, and Auckland on the eighth. Don't we have all this on our calendar?" I was curious to know why she was asking me all those dates when we had everything online.

But she seemed to pretend as if she didn't hear me. She asked, "You know Melissa's birthday is coming up, right? So what shall we do?"

"When is that?"

"Huh! I knew something was wrong. Now you can't even remember Melissa's birthday."

"Nothing is wrong, Jessie. You don't have to give me a memory test just because I forgot to tell you one thing. I'm doing that all the time myself. If my memory fails, you'll be the first to know."

"I don't want to know." Her voice cracked. "No, I think that came out wrong. What I mean is—"

"I know . . . I know." I tried to console her. "I'm not going anywhere just yet."

"Do you know that I live in constant fear? I can't even sleep at night. I'm always afraid a bad phone call will wake me up."

It was a lucky thing I hadn't delivered my speech at lunch the previous day. It would've made matters worse.

As she made a move to get up again, a teardrop slid down her cheek. She quickly wiped it off with a tissue and said, "Sorry about that."

I looked her in the eye and said, "I understand…sit here and let's talk. Why don't we talk anymore?" I wanted to tell her I was familiar with those scary thoughts all too well, but I couldn't let her sink. I had to make this better for her any way I could. I said, "What's the point in thinking about stuff that didn't happen? Instead of fearing for what we don't know, let's savor this moment in time. And let's celebrate every day we get."

"Amen to that." Jessie wiped the corners of her eyes.

I was about to continue, but I stopped as Melissa came in. "Are you guys staying in? If you are, I'll go have lunch and run a few errands. I'll be back in an hour."

"Sure, Melissa, we can hold down the fort for you until then." I looked at Jessie and asked, "Do you want to order something for lunch? Or I could go get sandwiches from downstairs."

"Sandwiches and coffee sound good to me. Melissa dear, would you mind ordering on your way out? Ask Linda to send it up," said Jessie.

"You got it," replied Melissa, and she left.

Jessie looked at me and asked, "Sorry, what were you saying?"

"Oops, I totally forgot."

Jessie looked at me and said, "Never mind. I have something to ask you."

"Shoot."

"What can we do to boost the senator's support for the bill? It's still very slow. So far, we've scheduled only five workshops in the US over the next three months."

"Are we missing something?"

"I can think of one thing," said Jessie.

"For heaven's sake, say it out loud, Jessie. We need to explore every possibility."

"I was thinking along the line of news coverage or something of that kind," suggested Jessie.

"You're right. There's still a huge chunk of people who don't look up everything on the internet. But why would any channel give us coverage? We have to think of an angle. I've heard that even PR agencies often have to pull strings," I said.

"That's where our Kim comes in. Remember Kim from our cheerleading team?"

"Sorry, I don't remember any Kim."

"It's Kimberley, silly. We girls used to call her Kim, but the guys used to call her 'Barely.' They teased her for being flat-chested and said she was barely a girl, and I guess that's how the name came about."

"Yes, I remember Barely. Who wouldn't? Everybody knew her in school. Anyway, what about her?"

"Now she works for a national news channel. What if we meet her one day? She would love to see you."

"Why me?"

"Because you were the smartest in our class. Everyone would be interested to know what the best student in the class has grown up to be."

"And they would be utterly disappointed."

"You think so? You think you would've done a better job being a heart surgeon? ... I'm shocked." Jessie looked disappointed. "Here's an opportunity to create history, and you think so little of it."

I didn't know how to explain my frustrations to her. I blurted out, "It's not that. You won't understand."

"Try me."

"I grew up thinking only one thing, and when that was so near, my dream just burst like a balloon. How would you feel? Frankly, I didn't choose this job; it just happened."

But Jessie reacted sharply. "First, if you think you're the only person who was denied a chosen career, think again. Besides, your life pushed you toward R&D, not to a fight for a 'Parental Fitness Test' movement. I always thought this was your choice." Then, she took one of the volunteer badges lying on my table, held it up on her chest like a medal, and said, "I don't know about you, but I'm proud to be a part of this movement. This makes me feel important and useful."

"I know. I think you're right." I understood what she was trying to say. "Let's call Barely."

"You can forget any coverage if you ever call her by that name. Besides, now she looks very different, so don't pass your judgment yet. I don't know what she did, but whatever it was, it worked. I haven't seen her for a long time; I've only seen her on Instagram and Facebook, but it seems she has grown into quite a woman."

A week later, we met Kimberley over dinner. It was a good meeting. Jessie and Kim had always been good friends, but Jessie had fallen off the grid after Lukas was diagnosed with hemophilia. None of her friends knew what she had been doing all this time. When Kim first heard from her, she was overjoyed. After hearing what she had been through and what she had undertaken, Kimberley said, "You were our team captain then, and you're still the leader. I am proud of you, Jessie. You should meet the rest of the team; they'll be so happy. We still try to meet at least once every three months. Remember who started that after we left school?"

Jessie and Kimberley had their girly chit-chat, but Kimberley had also grown and had become quite a professional. After hearing everything about our objectives and the website, she said, "I'm sure you know how TV stations work. I'll submit my initial findings and the story to my station director. Then, he has to get approval from the editor-in-chief. I can't make any promises, but I have a good feeling about this."

Chapter 16

A month later, we were getting ready for our sixth workshop in Canada, and this time, it was in Toronto. But Kimberley's silence for one month had really disappointed Jessie. "Not even a word? I don't believe it," said Jessie one day, a week ago. And just the day before the workshop, she mentioned it again. "This is the kind of event that needs national coverage. Next time I meet her, I will give her a piece of my mind."

"She may have her reasons." I tried to defend Kimberley—not that I was supporting her against Jessie, but I didn't want Jessie to feel bitter about her close friend.

"She could've at least told us so," Jessie argued.

"Don't worry. We have Patrick covering the show anyway, right?" Patrick, a local guy who was mostly known for shooting wedding videos and some seminars once in a while, had been recording our events since we had started our workshops.

"Sure…but we could've used national coverage to explore other cities later. You're right; now I know I can't depend on anybody. I'm gonna call Niven for coverage in the US for our next workshop. I think Niven is on Fox News now."

I was very sure I had never had made that comment about not depending on anyone. I had no idea where she'd got that from. But I decided to let it slide. We had a lot to prepare before we presented our case to the public of Toronto. The local guys had told us the turnout could be anywhere between three hundred and five hundred people.

We were surprised the moment we reached Stanley Park in the southern part of Toronto. Our volunteers there had convinced the mayor to let us host the event in the park with other festivities. It was a wonderful idea. Parents brought their kids, and it became a perfect day out. The local guys had also organized food and drink stalls at one side. The overall atmosphere was more fun than clinical.

Jessie was right. Although two or three reporters with their cameramen from the local news channels were already there, national coverage of such an event could've helped us a lot.

"Hi, David, do you know where I can find Jessie? Isn't she here yet?" someone asked me from behind as I was putting my cue cards in sequence.

"She's backstage," I answered without even looking. But moments later, I realized the lady had sounded a lot like Kimberly. Was that really her? *That's going to be a disaster.* Thinking how Jessie might react, I turned back to tell Kimberley that seeing Jessie before the show might not be a good idea, but she was already gone.

I managed to totally forget about the incident until I saw Kimberley again, just in front of the stage with her camera crew. I looked at Jessie at the other end of the stage, and I read her lips, silently saying, "I know."

Although I wanted to buy Kim and her crew dinner after the workshop was over, Kimberley said, "Sorry, it has to be another day, David. I gotta rush back to make it to nine o'clock news tonight." Then she looked at Jessie and said, "My friend here almost wrote me off. I'm sorry, dear. I apologize. I got the 'go ahead' just late last night."

"Maybe I shouldn't have flared up like that. I'm sorry too. We're good now?" Jessie hugged her.

"Absolutely. I'll call you." And Kim ran to the car.

Jessie turned to me and asked, "What do you think?"

"About what?"

"About the workshop, silly. Putting Christina and James on a video conference was a great idea. How did you get James to talk? I couldn't get more than a few polite words out of him in the last three months…but the kids loved him."

"He's a charismatic boy. What can I say? I felt James could help cheer up the kids. He's brave, and he's smart. He's the right person—not us—to inspire and help the children cope with their questions. After all, having a genetic disease isn't the end of the world, and he's the perfect example of that."

"Absolutely. He also gave them his email address. That's really nice of him," said Jessie.

By the time we packed up and reached our hotel, it was almost seven in the evening. Although our initial plan had been to go out for dinner to a restaurant in Toronto which Jessie's mother had raved about, after spending the whole day out on the field, room service sounded just great. There was also another reason: although we weren't sure whether Kimberley's piece would make it to the prime-time news that night, we were praying and hoping that it would.

In anticipation, we turned on the TV as soon as we finished our dinner. Unknowingly, we stopped talking and waited for the national news. I couldn't even remember when was the last time I had waited for the national news so eagerly—maybe never. Even the monotonous theme music struck a chord that day. As the news started, Jessie extended her left hand toward me, and I held it tight.

First came the headline news: "Our prime minister expressed Canada's willingness to accept more refugees from war-torn Syria." There was also more on the Ottawa shooting and on the Malaysia Airlines tragedy. Ten minutes passed and Jessie's grip loosened. She walked up to the minibar and said, "I need a drink. You want one?"

But Jessie turned back and ran to her seat as Kimberley's voice came on. And she cried out, "Where's my phone? Where's my phone?"

I picked it up from where she had been sitting earlier and handed it over to her. "Here you go; it slipped underneath your jacket."

She asked me to call her sister, Lucy, and she called Mrs. James herself. "Mom, turn on Channel 5 now."

Kimberley started off with the day's events in the park. She interviewed a few parents as they were enjoying a perfect day out with their kids. She captured the upbeat mood of the audience and parts of our speeches from the workshop. She rounded off with her own line. "It's not another organization asking for donations. They are only asking for your signature for a carrier screening test to make sure our kids don't suffer from inherited genetic diseases." With that, the camera closed in on James's face.

All-in-all it was four to five minutes' coverage—solid publicity on national TV. But we hit the jackpot when she promised her audience more. "Wait until I bring you another first—an exclusive interview with the organizers next week." Jessie and I both looked at each other, pleasantly surprised.

But as soon as the show was over, Jessie's phone rang, and she covered the phone with her left hand and whispered, "Hey, it's Kim."

Kim was doing the talking and Jessie was listening. I anxiously looked at Jessie's face and tried to read her expressions. She looked happy, with a big grin on her face. Minutes later, when she hung up, she threw her phone on the sofa, hugged me, and said, "Guess what? Her station wants an exclusive on the interview. She's coming to Calgary again tomorrow evening. She also told me not to talk to anybody, especially to any other rival stations, until she speaks with us again."

Jessie's phone rang again. This time, it was her mom. Soon after, Dr. Tyler called me to congratulate us. He had watched the news too.

Jessie's phone rang again. Jessie said, "It's Christina," as she picked up the call, and then my phone rang again, and for the next twenty minutes, we received phone calls one after another from our loved ones congratulating us on the coverage. However, Jessie's phone rang non-stop for the next two hours—calls from people she hadn't spoken to for months and years. Finally, she decided to put it on silent before going to bed because we had to catch an early morning flight.

Kimberley showed up at five the next evening. We were expecting her, so Jessie had bought Kim's favorite strawberry-cream mini donuts when she went out for lunch. But what we didn't expect was her camera crew. We had no idea she would be doing the interview the same evening. We hadn't prepared ourselves for anything. But Kim said, "I don't want a scripted interview. Besides, you guys are so passionate about the whole issue, I didn't think you needed any preparations. Just ignore the camera and everything will be fine."

Soon, Kim and her team turned our small office into a studio, with high-powered lights, reflectors, and cameras everywhere. Kimberley didn't want to waste any time. She told her crew to prepare us for the shoot. Who knew they also had a makeup girl with them? We were a little confused at first, but we played along because we both knew what the interview could do for our campaign.

Kimberley explained. "TV producers are like sharks. If they smell news, they'll do whatever they need to." She didn't want to take any chances. She had to get things rolling before someone else did.

When we watched the telecast later that week, I told Jessie, "The interview came out even better than the first TV coverage." It was all about the voluntary parental fitness test: how a simple carrier screening test could change the face of genetic diseases for the future generation, how we had started, and how we had come this far, and all about the people behind the scene. In simple words, Kimberly made our close to one year's efforts nationally known within one week. And signatures for voluntary carrier screening tests came pouring in from all over Canada.

We were flooded with calls and emails. And to top it all, the following week, the same program was aired again in the US. Kimberley didn't tell us anything about that; I heard about it from the senator. He had been keeping a close watch on our progress, and he had become a part of our movement since the day we'd met.

But his call on a Saturday evening took me by surprise at first. Jessie and I were out for dinner. He called me as soon as the program went live on television in the US. Since he had already seen the show, he wasn't interested in the telecast; he was more interested in discussing what that TV exposure could do to garner support in the US. He said, "Let's meet next week. Can you guys come to New York?" Then he paused and came back on after a few seconds. "But hang on, this part they're showing now is the Hartford workshop. How did they do that?"

"I have no idea, sir. But they did ask us for old footage from our previous workshops, and we made copies for them."

"Well done, guys, but we need to move fast. See you next week. Now go enjoy your dinner."

Jessie was looking at my face, trying to read what was going on. I had said very little; it was him doing the talking, making it difficult for her to understand anything. So I went through the conversation all over again.

The next week, when we met the senator in his New York office, he looked like a different man. I knew he was an accomplished and influential senator, but I never took him to be a tech-savvy strategist. He had a dozen other computer and research geeks with him in that room. I saw Dr. Edward sitting at one corner of the big table. He welcomed us with a big smile and a warm "hello." He looked pleased with our progress.

But the senator was in no mood for idle chit-chat. He started in immediately. "As I said earlier, introducing a mandatory carrier screening test won't be easy. We need to build a strong public opinion first. I like what you're doing in Canada. Let's do more workshops in the US. We need more senators on board."

Everyone was listening to the senator, though his tech team was glued to their laptop screens. I had no idea what they were typing away at. Suddenly, I heard Jessie's voice. "Sir, even if we reach out to two states per month, that'll take us a minimum of two years to get close to all of them and to build a solid network."

I shivered in panic. *Do I have two years?* Thank god, Senator Ruth had a way out.

"You're right, Jessie. But maybe there's another way to do it. You don't have to go to each and every congressman and woman; you need to convince only the most senior and the influential party members. You set up a workshop in their own constituencies and let them see the reactions on the ground. My team here has dissected the whole country into sixteen must-do areas for you," said Senator Ruth, and a US map popped up on the big screen, divided into sixteen parts with sixteen senators' name on it. "Lydia, now zoom in on any one zone." The senator turned to one young lady on his right.

Dr. Edward said, "If we work fast, maybe we can introduce the bill to the Senate and get it assigned to a committee within a year from now." And he looked at the senator for support.

"I would say, one year is doable," said the senator.

I saw some light again. I wanted to get this done before I took to my bed, but I realized this wouldn't be easy. Opposition against our efforts was also mounting up. Since the TV broadcast, accusations and condemnations had gone up. The voice against mandatory carrier screening tests was getting louder. Still, we couldn't stop. I said, "Tell us what you want us to do."

The senator looked at me and said, "We need you guys to be here for the next two months. To introduce the bill in one year, we have to have these sixteen senators on board within the first two months. Then, we give them two to three months to talk to their close supporters. I'll sponsor the bill, but as you all know, more co-sponsors will increase our chances. So what do you say?"

"We would love to, sir, but moving here for two months will be rather difficult. We have no one else in our Calgary office. Locally, we're running a few support groups, and we have our regular visits to hospitals and OB/GYN providers. We're trying hard to convince them to offer a carrier screening test to everyone in the preconception period. We think that's going to help us in a big way. Besides, people from other parts of the world also look to us for all kinds of support."

The senator's eyes turned cold, and his face got a look of sheer disbelief. He told his team to take a break, and they all disappeared. Then he looked at Dr. Edward and said, "The thing is, without strong public opinion, we can't push this thing through. We need you guys to be more active in the US."

"Don't worry, senator, we'll make it work. We're committed to this," assured Dr. Edward.

"Well then, why don't we reconvene at the same time tomorrow? I have another engagement a little later. I want you guys to know I'm here to help. But before I go public, we must have the ground covered. We need a strong public opinion in place."

"Don't worry. We'll work something out and have a solution by tomorrow," said Dr. Edward, and we left the senator's office.

And with that next-day morning commitment, our plan to get back to Calgary by an evening flight had also gone out the window. We walked to Dr. Edward's office to find a solution. His office was just a couple of blocks away. Outside, it was pleasant and sunny, so we'd a nice walk. As soon as we settled down in another big conference room, his secretary brought us coffee and some donuts. I presumed that was our lunch.

I was still thinking about what the senator had just said. How could we leave everything in Calgary and move to the US for two months? Reaching out to those sixteen senators was important, and of course, we couldn't ask Senator Ruth to slow down just because we didn't have more people to help. That would be very unprofessional. Besides, if we had to reject his proposal, a mandatory carrier screening test would be as good as dead in the United States. It would never see the light of success anytime soon.

Still, how could we disappoint our members and volunteers from other parts of the world? If we disappeared for two months, that would be suicide for our voluntary carrier screening test campaign. We had over one million people who had already pledged themselves to voluntary carrier screening tests. We all had only one goal; to turn that million into a billion. We all knew signatures for a voluntary test was a slow process, but that was the only ammunition we had in our arsenal, and it was building up. We were hoping that family by family, one day, we would be able to wipe out those diseases from the human gene pool.

Now that movement could go on with or without me. How could I gamble with that? On the other hand, having the bill in the US might help the concept achieve greater recognition and worldwide awareness, making it seem more serious and assist in the worldwide outreach. If so, then the pause might be totally worth it, and, if successful, the bill might more than make up for the break, through the momentum afterward.

I came back to my senses as Dr. Edward walked into the conference room and said, "Give me something, guys., We can't just say 'no' to the senator. Don't forget, he's doing this for us."

Jessie said, "We know, but we don't have enough people, sir."

"Right. But you have to think of something. Don't you have anybody on your team who can back you up for a month or two in Calgary? How about that Melissa lady?"

"She's new, sir," said Jessie.

The first person who came to my mind was Christina. "How about Christina? She might help us," I said out loud.

But Jessie said it would be impossible for her to help, even if she wanted to. "They all want to help us, but these parents are fighting hard for their own battles. They're stretched to the limit. They don't have time to help anybody."

I asked, "How about Kelly or Susan in New York? Can one of them take our place?"

"You aren't thinking." She gave me a rundown of their daily routine from morning until night.

I wasn't the only one impressed by Jessie's remark. Dr. Edward said, "It's this kind of involvement that makes any social organization tick. I'm glad you guys stay so close to your members. Good work, Jessie."

"Thank you, sir." Jessie smiled.

Dr. Edward said, "But I'm running out of options and time. I'm going to propose something here you guys might not like."

We both looked at his face and waited in anticipation. Dr. Edward took a sip of his coffee and asked, "What happens if you two split up? One of you can stay in Calgary, and the other person goes on tour."

Dr. Edward's words came like a bombshell to me. I didn't know what to say. I wasn't a public speaker. Australia and New Zealand were different; I had had only one workshop in each country. But we were planning fifteen to twenty workshops in the US. I couldn't do that on my own. And Jessie might be embarrassed if she had to face questions about any particular genetic disorder. No one could pre-empt the questions from a live audience. I couldn't put her in a situation like that.

I sat there silently for a while. The big clock on the wall kept ticking. Up until that time, I didn't even notice they had a clock on one side of the wall. I wanted to focus my attention on the immediate problems at hand, but the sound from the clock dragged me away. How could I stop that? *We all know time is fleeting, but do we need a crude reminder—tick-tock, tick-tock, tick-tock—every second of our lives?*

I suddenly woke up at Jessie's answer. "I don't think I can handle the workshops on my own, sir. As you know, I'm not qualified to answer many questions. Besides, I can't leave my son for two months, but I can look after the Calgary office with Melissa."

"Well, that's settled then. Thank you, Jessie…although you guys can talk about it and let us have your final decision by tomorrow morning. Let's go and meet the senator at eleven. I'll get you guys re-booked on the three o'clock flight."

"See you tomorrow," said Jessie. Then we shook hands and left.

"What was that?" I asked Jessie as soon as we stepped out of the building on 47th Street.

"What was what? You sat there saying nothing. Someone had to say something. And what's wrong with what I said?"

"Nothing. You just pushed the whole thing to me."

"What are you talking about? Tell me who is more qualified to talk?"

"You know qualification has nothing to do with this. I'm not a public speaker."

"Apparently, now you are." She giggled.

Later that evening, when we were having dinner at the restaurant downstairs in the hotel, I received a call from Dr. Edward. I showed Jessie his name on the screen, and I stepped outside to take the call.

"Sorry to bother you guys again." Dr. Edward's voice sounded worried.

"It's no bother, sir. What is it?"

"The senator doesn't think splitting you guys is the best solution. After a half-an-hour discussion, now I agree with him. Together, you guys are more effective. What do you think?"

I was sure if he could see my face at that moment, he wouldn't have had to ask me that question. I said, "Sir, we are perfectly okay with whatever you guys decide. Give me some time to think; we'll find a solution."

Dr. Edward sounded relieved and said, "Well, then, you guys think of something and let us know by early next week. I'll convey the change of plans to the senator. If you need to add manpower, we'll arrange for additional funding. Keep me posted."

When I came back to the table, Jessie asked, "What are you smiling about?"

After hearing everything, Jessie said, "Finally. Well, let's go back home and think. I'm exhausted."

We reached Calgary the next day. The sudden and eager change in direction from the senator had put us in an awkward situation. We couldn't just drop everything and move to the US for two months. But I also knew opportunities like that wouldn't come knocking every day. One of the most influential senators in the US had offered his help. If nothing else came of it, this could take our carrier screening test awareness program to the American heartlands. Besides, if the bill was passed in the US, that would set a positive precedent, and I could happily embrace the onset of the disease.

Jessie said, "I don't think we have much choice here. It will be a disaster if we say 'no' to his proposal. I can't even imagine that. Let's put our heads together and see if we can come up with any viable solution. After all, they both offered to help, didn't they?"

"Yes, they did, but we also have to think of it from every angle. First off, we wouldn't be staying in any one place for more than two to three days. We'd have to live out of our suitcases for two months."

Jessie said, "I'm not worried about ourselves. We can rough it out, but who will look after Lukas? I can't abandon him for two months. That's way too long. We've never lived separately like that before."

"You're right. Lukas is our number one concern. My other major worry is our members from all over the world; they need us as much as we need them. Although getting the bill passed in the US would be a big impetus to all, we can't ignore our present members. How can we attend to them when we're on the road twenty-four hours a day? Remember, even if the bill fails in the US, the voluntary carrier screening test is truly happening. If parents keep asking for the test, soon the OB/GYN providers will notice the change in the public mood. We can't jeopardize that."

Jessie held my hand and said, "I know…I know. But there must be a way out, right?"

"Maybe. But I can't think of one yet," I blurted out.

Two days went by without any progress. After a second day in the office with no solution in sight, Jessie said, "Come to my place and have a drink. Maybe we aren't seeing something. A change of scene might help."

I had nothing better to offer, and we needed an answer soon so that we could draw up a plan for the weekend meeting. This time, instead of us flying there, Dr. Edward and the senator wanted to come to Calgary to see our activities first-hand.

I followed Jessie into the house. Not so long ago, I had spent so much time there, but since we had moved to our new office, I hardly had any time to visit them.

"Hi, Mrs. James! How are you?" I asked as I met her at the door. Jessie headed upstairs to see Lukas.

"I'm fine. It's good to see you again. Tell me what you guys are up to now. Jessie hardly talks. She always says she's busy. Tell me, who isn't?" complained Mrs. James in one breath.

"You're right, Mrs. James."

Suddenly, we heard Jessie's voice from the next room. "Wine for you, Mom?"

"Sure." Then, Mrs. James lowered her voice and asked me, "But what are we celebrating?"

"Nothing. We're kind of stuck." I told her about our problem. She wasn't new to our organization or to our problems. In fact, she had been with us from the beginning. When Jessie came in and sat down, she filled in the rest.

Mrs. James said, "You guys are too close to the issue; you aren't seeing things straight. Haven't you heard of a 'Mobile Office'? You can take your office with you wherever you go. Rent an RV for a month instead of hopping from one hotel to the other. Then you can move into a hotel when necessary."

I agreed. "That's brilliant, Mrs. James. Thank you. Why didn't we think of that?"

"Wow, Mom! What a relief! That will also save us from packing and unpacking every other day—a total waste of time."

"Then we can also take Melissa with us," I said out loud.

Jessie's eyes lit up. "Can we? That would be great."

I added, "Let's take on help from an agency to look after the front office, and with our landlines transferred to mobile phones, no one will even notice we're gone."

"That's just perfect," said Jessie. She got up and took the empty glasses from us to refill. "Now we're getting somewhere. But we're still stuck with our number one problem: I can't leave Lukas for two months." She looked at her mother and asked, "Who will look after him during the day when you're at the office?"

"I can take unpaid leave for two months and be with him," answered Mrs. James promptly.

"I can't ask you to do that," said Jessie.

"You aren't asking, I am offering. It's my choice. I love to spend time with him. Besides, don't forget, I'm a part of this project too. I guess I'll be doing my part here."

I looked at Jessie and said, "Now that we have access to additional funds, we can compensate her partially."

"That won't be necessary," replied Mrs. James.

"Why not? Please, Mom?" Then, Jessie leaned toward her mother and wrapped her arms around her. "Thank you for doing this, Mom."

"Jessie, let me go. This is too much already." Mrs. James struggled to break free.

With our main worry out of the way, the next day I went straight to the hospital to see Dr. Tyler again. I hadn't seen him in the last few months, and I wanted to get his views on our plan. As Mrs. James had pointed out, when we're too deep in any situation, we don't see the solutions ourselves; we need another person looking out for us. And Dr. Tyler had always been that person for me. His secretary, Alice, smiled as soon as she saw me. "You're a lucky guy; he just came back from the class. Go right in."

As I was about to knock on the door, I saw Dr. Tyler coming out.

"Are you going out, sir?" I asked.

"Not yet. I came out to ask for a cup of coffee. What are you doing here?" Then he looked at Alice and said, "Make it two."

I followed him inside and told him all about the recent developments and what we were about to take up for the next two months. After hearing everything, he asked, "Can you guys stay on the roads for two months? It will be grueling."

"But this is our do-or-die moment, sir. If we miss this opportunity, it might be gone for a long time. And I'm afraid that's one thing I don't have."

"I understand your sentiment, son. Just be careful out there. Whether this bill is approved in the US or not, no one can take back what you guys have already achieved in one year. You definitely can't expect everyone to be enthusiastic about the bill. People usually don't like compulsions or government interferences in their lives. But hey, you have over one million people worldwide who have signed up for voluntary carrier screening tests. Do you know what that means? That means the program has given a head start to one million people with their test results. Now they can exercise their options. The program has wiped out the fear of passing on the genetic diseases from the minds of these people. And more importantly, it has done so without any medication. No one has achieved that to date. The program shows us the power of knowledge and awareness."

After leaving the hospital, I went straight to the office. Energized and encouraged by Dr. Tyler's comments, I was ready to take to the road. Thank god, we had people like Dr. Tyler and Mrs. James behind us.

The next day, on a conference call to Dr. Edward and the senator, we told them our plan. The senator said, "I like it; it sounds a lot like my campaign tour. Let's get the show on the road."

Chapter 17

On a Sunday morning, we all gathered at the senator's second home in New York at nine. He had inherited that property from his parents. Senator Ruth not only had arranged for a very comfortable RV, but he also had sacrificed the two most efficient workers from his team, Joe and Lydia, for the next two months. We hadn't seen them since our last meeting at the senator's office, and Lydia had an encouraging proposition for us; she said if we followed her itinerary, we should be able to wrap up the whole tour within the next forty-five days.

The senator added, "These two have followed me on several campaign trails. They know these senators well, and they'll brief you about each one before you meet them, telling you what the senators want to hear and what they don't. You guys do your thing and let them do theirs. I see a perfect five here; I can't think of a better team. Now, go get 'em!"

After breakfast, we started on our journey in a big American RV. I had never imagined an RV could be so very comfortable and roomy. If it wasn't on wheels, I could've mistaken it for someone's home. The girls took the bedroom at the back of the RV while Joe and I took two couches that folded down into beds in the living room area. The living room was also furnished with a TV and a music system. Lydia said, "This one is even better than the last RV we used during the campaign, right, Joe?"

Joseph was our designated driver. He blamed the distortion of his name to 'Joe' on American laziness. "Can you believe it? They don't even want to say my full name," complained Joseph.

But he wasn't bitter about it. He said, "That's the way it is." Joseph was about my age, but he preferred to call me "Doc." Apparently, Lydia liked that too, and Melissa followed. Occasionally, Jessie also teased me with the new nickname.

Melissa, Jessie, and I had worked together in our Calgary office for about six months, so we knew our individual duties. Although we didn't know at first what Lydia and Joseph would be doing, their roles became clear within the next few hours.

Joseph took charge of the RV and all our daily needs. Lydia was the point person for the senator contacts. She said, "You don't have to clutter your heads with information about all sixteen senators. All we have to do is convince one person at a time." And she pulled up that US map again with those sixteen senators' name on it. "Just as Senator Ruth is sending us to influence his contacts, these sixteen senators will reach out to their close congressmen and congresswomen to do the same."

Although at first, I didn't quite understand the rush, Lydia explained, "If we miss them in this August recess period, we won't be able to catch so many senators in their constituencies until next year, because they'll be back in DC. And it's important for them to see, firsthand, how their people respond to the information."

That was exactly what Senator Ruth had said. He wanted those senators to see the effect of the workshops in their home states. Lydia must've spent hours creating that itinerary.

Lydia continued. "Each senator has their pet projects. We just have to make sure we don't step on any toes. Tomorrow, I'll brief you on our first target area under Senator Bobby Matos. We will meet him in Cleveland, but besides Ohio, we can also leave a few other states under his care."

After that brief meeting, I sat next to Joseph in the co-pilot's seat. The feeling was incredible. I had never felt so free in my whole life. The clear blue skies and the miles and miles of open roads had an alluring effect. I understood the reason behind America's obsession with road trips. It was intoxicating. As we left behind the shiny city towers and the lingering suburbia, Joe put on some country music. It was just the thing we needed.

At first, I didn't quite grasp what Lydia meant when she had said we should be able to cover all sixteen senators within the next forty-five days if we followed her itinerary. A week later, as we wrapped things up in Missouri, she told Joseph and Melissa to take the RV to Houston and wait until we got there. Then, she looked at Jessie and said, "Pack for four days. We'll take a flight to Seattle from here, and then to Sacramento."

That was a smart choice. Why drive such long distances to catch two senators at two ends? But I guess my silence confused Lydia. She asked, "Anything to add, Doc?"

I replied, "Not really," and I realized Lydia's plan had just saved us at least six to seven days. Lydia was smart, and she had planned our route in such a manner that we never drove if we didn't have a stop within a hundred miles. Flying to those far-off destinations was definitely the wisest thing to do.

And that was just the beginning. One by one, we met all sixteen senators and managed to conduct all our scheduled workshops successfully wherever we stopped. Thank god, we didn't have to take the RV everywhere. That would've easily taken us two to three more weeks.

When we had started off, I was very nervous about those roadshows because most Americans would be hearing us, or even about us, for the first time in their lives. But it turned out people were waiting for us with flower bouquets, banners, and streamers. We were swayed by the heartfelt warmth and the great hospitality. Some even invited us to their homes. One common problem had created an inseparable bond between all of us. As we moved from one town to the next, stopping the inherited genetic diseases didn't look like an absurd idea anymore. It could be a reality soon—within our reach, without having to wait for any further FDA approval. I was thrilled.

We received loud applause whenever we pulled up our real-time numbers. Everybody screamed. One and a quarter million people, and still counting, had already signed up for voluntary carrier screening tests. And while showing that, every time, I repeated Dr. Tyler's line: "What this means is that the program has already wiped out the fear of passing on genetic diseases from more than one million people. And it has effectively done so without any medication." They cheered.

Nonetheless, it wasn't all good. There were hiccups at a few points. We met with our first major protest in front of the Missouri venue. But after my bad experience at the Hartford Community Hall, this time, I didn't want to ignore them. I got out of the rental car and asked the rest of the team members to go inside and go ahead with the preparations. Jessie said, "Let me get down, too."

"Don't worry, it'll only take a few minutes. I'll call you if I need anything."

There were about eighteen or twenty of them, holding a few placards and chanting slogans that expressed their grievances against our carrier screening test campaign. From the

look of it, I assumed the guy addressing his fellow protesters must be the leader. I walked up to him and introduced myself.

He said, "I'm Billy," and he chanted again, "Down with the carrier screening test." The rest followed.

I said, "Can we talk?"

He looked at me again and said, "Of course…are you withdrawing the workshop?"

"That depends. Why don't you all come inside and let's continue this conversation?"

"Sorry, there's nothing to talk about. We don't want to leave the protest."

"Well then, why don't you come inside with one of your members?"

He told the rest to continue chanting until they heard from him, and we went inside. I wasn't quite familiar with the venue myself, so I asked one of the organizers whether he could show us to a small room where we could talk privately.

I didn't have much time on hand. I asked Billy, "Do you know what this is all about?"

He said, "Yes, this is anti-procreation. This is against God's will."

I protested. "I certainly don't know what God wants, but a carrier screening test isn't really anti-procreation."

"Well, that's one man's opinion," answered Billy curtly.

"Okay, let's forget carrier screening tests for a minute. Do you help out at shelters and give money and clothes to the homeless?"

"I try. But what's your point?"

"Then tell me 'why.' Why do you want to help others?"

"You're really weird, man. Are you human or not? Don't you feel anything for them?"

"Of course, I do. But I also feel for these kids." I opened my laptop and showed him some of our picture files of the member families and told him how they were robbed of the simple pleasures of life. "In fact, we aren't asking anyone to stop giving birth—we're offering a precautionary measure. I don't see you protesting in front of outlets selling birth control pills or condoms. Why?"

"Aren't condoms for protection?" Billy asked hesitantly.

"Exactly. Likewise, carrier screening tests can also protect our future kids from inheriting deadly genetic diseases. In fact, we aren't proposing anything new; we're only asking parents to take the test. Why is that so bad?"

"But if the government makes it a law, wouldn't that be binding on everyone? Then, where is the choice?" asked Billy.

"You're right. You have a point there. Recently, I have been thinking about that, too. You know how you roll out something, thinking you've got everything covered, and then you realize your offering is far from perfect. You still need to fine-tune and fix things, much like the updates we receive for Windows. I think the mandatory testing is one such bug in the movement that needs to be fixed."

"You think so?" Billy asked in a surprised voice.

"I do. If you can trust me, give me two months and your contact numbers, and I will get back to you on this. I would love to keep the testing voluntary."

Billy seemed to realize I meant every word I said, and they all packed up after that meeting. In fact, I had been thinking about keeping the test voluntary since I had met Andy, at the very start of the road trip, in Cleveland.

Andy had said, "Everyone wants the freedom to choose. On one hand, carrier screening tests give us the freedom to choose—after the test, we can pray for a miracle and hope that everything will go our way, or we can look for alternatives like gene editing, if available, or adoption. But it stifles us the moment it becomes mandatory."

So when I saw the picketing in front of the Missouri auditorium, I didn't want to avoid them. I wanted to see how they would react if we made the program voluntary. And after the workshop, I asked Jessie, "What do you think?"

"Didn't you want everyone to take the test?" said Jessie.

"Yes, but now I am re-thinking it. Maybe we shouldn't force it on people. We started off with the idea of informing people about the already available carrier screening tests. Didn't we? All we wanted was for parents to know that they could stop it from passing on to their kids if they wanted to. It was all about making an informed decision. Maybe we went a little overboard?"

"That's probably right," answered Jessie calmly, "but what do we tell the senator now? I'm sure he won't like it."

"Let's finish what we came here to do. I'll talk to the senator later."

The second disturbance came when I was delivering my speech at our workshop in Omaha, Nebraska. A lady named Suzanne suddenly got up from the audience and asked me, "Who are you... playing Bruce Almighty? What makes you think you can't have a fulfilling life with a genetic disease?"

If anyone had asked me such questions a month before, I probably would've considered it a setback. But I had learned a lot since then. I had realized I couldn't ignore anyone's voice; they were all part of this movement.

I looked at the lady and said, "Let me answer your questions right away. By the way, I'm David. And you are...?"

"I'm Suzanne," said the lady. Although her voice didn't reach me, the crowd around her helped to deliver the name to the stage.

"Well, Suzanne, you've asked two questions. Let me answer the first one first. To tell you frankly, I'm not playing God or any Bruce Almighty. You know why?"

By that time someone had handed over a microphone to her. She asked, "Why?"

"Because we have no intention to play with anyone's will-power. Remember, even your Bruce Almighty had to give up at the end?" The audience laughed.

I continued. "All we are asking is for parents to take a carrier screening test so that their children don't suffer from genetic diseases that have no treatment yet. You may have noticed that not all family physicians and OB/GYN providers are offering the test in the preconception period. Why? We're here to help you get that.

"When someone lends a hand to an elderly person to help him cross a busy road or gives food to anyone hungry and poor, do you think that person is interfering with God's work?"

"Of course not. But that's different," answered Suzanne.

"Actually, it's not much different. Now, let me give you an example closer to our kind of work. If we had left diseases like cholera and tuberculosis untreated and never took steps to prevent or eradicate those diseases, half the population would have been dead by now. Did the scientists and the doctors play God then?

"Have you heard of an organization called Doctors Without Borders? They help people where no one else will help. They treat everything from war-wounds to epidemics. Tell me, should they have left the victims alone as God's will?"

I looked at her and waited a couple of seconds in case she had something to say. Then I continued. "Now, what we're asking is for people to take the test so that they can make an informed decision. We aren't here to influence your decision in any way. We just want you to know what you're up against and what the other alternatives are available to you." I paused and then asked Suzanne, "Did I answer your first question?"

"Yes, you did. Thank you."

"Now, to answer your second question," I started again. "I can proudly say I've seen most of my friends fighting genetic diseases themselves or at home, but that hasn't taken their smiles away. In fact, most of them are stronger and more organized than usual. They lead a very happy life. But that's not to say they don't cry. Look at me. I'm HD positive, and there's no cure for that yet, but do I think my life is wasted? No way. I love what I'm doing. My purpose here is to see that the future kids don't have to live in fear every day like I do."

Suzanne didn't say another word. She didn't have to. It seemed the overwhelming support from the audience had silenced any opposition for a while. Considering the uphill battle we were fighting, the whole trip could be considered successful. At least, that's what Senator Ruth said when I told him about the disruptions on the phone. However, I knew in my heart that the opposition was far from over, and it was time we saw things from their point of view, too.

I had never traveled a long distance by road before. What was pretty normal for most families throughout North America had always been missing in my life. I knew we had our constraints, so I was glad I had made that trip. I realized what road trips were all about, and I got a taste of real America—the heart and soul.

I was convinced that the parents who had experienced the darkness of any genetic disease were ready to sign on the dotted lines, and they weren't alone. At the end of our tour, the voluntary carrier screening test numbers for parental fitness had crossed more than two million signatures, with seven hundred thousand added in the US alone since we had started the roadshows. I was glad we took to the road.

Sixteen hundred miles and forty-six days later, we flew back home on a Tuesday afternoon. Mrs. James opened the door with a big smile.

As we all sat down, Mrs. James told us what had happened in Calgary in the last one and a half months. Everything was pretty much the same as expected, except for one thing. She looked at Jessie and said in a solemn voice, "Dylan is back."

And that marked the end of my uninterrupted six months with Jessie. It had actually been more than eight months since Dylan last left. I remembered a few days before Jessie had complained about it. "See how irresponsible Dylan is? He never even called to inform me that he would be delayed. Lukas has already asked me three times, 'When is Dad coming back?' He can't keep him waiting like this. I think this time he's gone for good."

Although Jessie had spoken with Lukas and her mother frequently on the phone during our road trip, I was surprised that Mrs. James hadn't mentioned Dylan's return to her before. Jessie looked at her mother and blurted out, "That bastard! What does he want now?"

"Jessie!" shouted Mrs. James in a stern voice. "Language. Don't forget you're a mother now."

"When did he come back? Where is he? Why didn't you tell me?" Jessie went non-stop.

Mrs. James stopped her. "I didn't think you could do much from there. Besides, whether you like it or not, he's still the father of your son. And to answer your other questions, he came two days ago, and he's staying at the Plaza."

Jessie kept quiet for a few seconds; she must've realized she had made a mistake. She walked up to Mrs. James and apologized for the outburst. She came back to the sofa and sat down in exasperation. I had never seen Jessie so restless. I didn't know how I could help. I said, "Why don't you go have a bath and relax? Deal with all that later."

"I can't relax now. I know what I have to do first."

"What's that?"

Jessie didn't answer my question. She got up again, picked up her purse, took the car key, and left. On her way out, she looked at me and said, "Don't wait up. I'll catch up in the office tomorrow."

Mrs. James quickly followed her and asked from the open doorway as Jessie walked to the car, "Where are you going?"

"To end this charade." And she drove away.

I left soon after, and although I was dying to know what she meant by "ending this charade," I didn't get a chance to ask her anything throughout the day.

When I went to bed at night, one line was still ringing in my head: "To end this charade." *What did she mean by that? What was she going to tell Dylan now?* Jessie had already told me she only tolerated Dylan for Lukas's sake, and she had no plan to get back together. Meanwhile, she had also told Lukas what his father had offered, but Lukas said he didn't want to go to London, either. So was this about the divorce papers? Or was it about his disruptive visits now and then in Lukas's life? In a way, it disrupted her life, too.

But this time, unlike when I'd returned from my trip to Australia, I hadn't prepared any speech for Jessie —because I wasn't going to deliver one and walk away from Jessie's life. The uninterrupted last eight months with Jessie had taught me something important, and I realized I could have the same uninterrupted time for the rest of my life. So what if it was short? If Dylan's visit meant a fight, a fight it would be.

The next day, being the first day back after an absence of almost one and a half months, involved a lot of catching up. The whole day, we had no time to talk about our own situation, but Jessie summed up everything in one line. She texted: "I got his signature, and I'm free."

I thanked God, for I wasn't much of a fighter. Then I tried to concentrate on my work. Although we had worked from the RV, we hadn't been able to achieve much. We'd had to spend a lot of time preparing for the ongoing workshops, and we'd only managed to attend to urgent matters. We had pushed aside the rest. Naturally, the work was piling up.

After coming back, we immediately added one more person to our team—Irfan—to bear the additional workload. Irfan was in his early twenties, and he spoke four languages. Besides English, he was also fluent in German, French, and Spanish. That kind of language skill could be of great help in our campaign in Europe.

Until about two months ago, our focus had been in Europe. But our workshops in America's heartlands and the senator's aggressive stance had changed all that. Making carrier screening tests mandatory looked closer than ever. Everyone in Europe also thought taking the fight to the heartlands was a great idea. "Can we do that here?" asked Robin from Copenhagen.

Some other volunteers in Europe also wanted to emulate the same idea in their respective countries as soon as possible. However, there seemed to be a major difference in the European outlook. Most members cared little about the legalities. They only wanted people to exercise their choice—that was all; they weren't keen to push it to be legally binding. And that sentiment was working.

Since our workshop in Cleveland, I was also leaning toward that school of thought. Making carrier screening tests compulsory to prove parental fitness wasn't sitting too well with me. And Dr. Tyler's words kept recurring in my mind. He had already warned me about people's mindset where governmental interference was concerned. Obviously, people should have the freedom to choose. *After all, we're no lawmakers.*

A week later, I realized I wouldn't be able to move forward until I discussed the issue with Dr. Edward and the senator. And we owed them a visit anyway. Since we had finished the road trip earlier than scheduled and they weren't available to meet us at that time, we flew back home. Jessie had already said she had no problem with keeping the program voluntary, but she was worried about how the senator would take it.

I immediately went to Jessie's office and said, "I know you're tied up here, but I'm planning to fly to New York tomorrow to brief them about our trip. I also intend to explain why we should keep ourselves out of politics and the lawmaking decisions in any country. Are you okay with that?"

"Sure. I hope they don't mind the change in direction, although to think of it, it's not really much of a change. We have always campaigned on our website for voluntary carrier screening tests for parental fitness. There was no compulsion."

"Exactly," I said.

"But you just came back from such a long trip. Don't you need to rest for a few days?" asked Jessie.

"I can't rest until I finish two very important things on my to-do list. And this is one of them."

"What's the other one?" Jessie asked.

"I'll tell you as soon as this one is over."

The next day, I reached New York in the evening and met with Dr. Edward and the senator the following day. This was our first meeting after the road trip. Naturally, they were both very eager to see me, although, at first, they were a bit surprised to see me alone.

Dr. Edward quickly apologized for not being able to meet us when we came back after the road trip. He said, "I was in Zurich. Anyway, how are you? How is Jessie?" Dr. Edward sounded really concerned.

"We're all fine, sir. Thank you. We just got back to Calgary a week ago, so it was difficult for Jessie to leave town again."

"We understand. Tell us about the road trip," said the senator.

"It was amazing. I have to say, it was unlike anything I have ever experienced before. I learned a lot."

"Road trips always teach us new things. But Melissa said you had something very urgent to talk about. What is it?" asked the senator.

Then I briefly told them about the main events of the trip, sharing every bit of my conversations with the picketers and protesters. I asked, "May I speak freely, sir?"

The senator said, "Of course, David." Dr. Edward nodded.

I looked at the senator and continued. "You were right from day one, sir: we can't force a decision on people. My feeling is that as a social organization, we are stronger if we work independently, without any political entanglements. People will be more receptive. The problem seems to arise from the moment we campaign carrier screening tests to be mandatory. Otherwise, the program can simply educate people about genetic diseases and offer a choice, while providing support and solidarity among those who already have such diseases. I don't think generating public opinion should be our objective, and I don't think it ever was. If we simply push for voluntary carrier screening tests first, we can break the anti-procreation divide and can get more people to support us. And based on that support and numbers, someday, if any country decides to make carrier screening tests legally binding, it should be a matter of public debate for them. If you ask me, we aren't there yet in the US or anywhere in the world."

"Are you sure this will make such a big difference to that section of people?" asked Dr. Edward.

"Let me give you an example, sir. Will anyone object to any organization distributing condoms in a neighborhood to promote safe sex? Probably not. Because using the condom will always be up to the user. And once the benefits of the condoms are established, the users will embrace it. Would condoms be such a popular choice if they had been mandatory? I fear that even its avid supporters would have objected to the rule just because it infringes on personal choice and personal freedom."

Dr. Edward and the senator both looked at me and kept quiet for a few seconds, but to me, each second felt like an hour. Looking at Dr. Edward's face, I felt he had had a shock. However, the senator broke the silence first. "This is your project, David. Remember what I told you the first day I met you? 'We're here to help,' and I meant it. You're the boss. If you think this is the best way to move forward, I'm fine with that."

Dr. Edward turned to the senator and said, "I'm sorry, senator."

"Me too," I said. "Maybe I was too emotional and overwhelmed by our own conditions at that time and got carried away."

The senator said, "What are you guys 'sorry' about? I think David is right. We aren't there yet. I'm surprised he could feel the pulse of the people in two months when it can take politicians years to learn that. Besides, as David said, we need to debate, and I don't know whether you guys have noticed it or not, the campaign has already sparked a debate."

"What do we do now?" I asked.

"We do exactly what we have been doing, with some modifications as you've now suggested. You guys do your workshops in the US as you do it in any other country. If house representatives and senators aren't involved in your campaign, you guys automatically remain apolitical. Let's build awareness first. Some parents will always reject testing based on their faith and philosophy, but that's different from not being tested for lack of awareness that such a test exists in the first place."

"My point exactly, sir. But we will miss you, Senator"

"I'm not going anywhere. If you don't mind, I would still like to be a part of the movement in my personal capacity. Let me know if you guys need any help here."

"I'd like that very much, sir."

On my way to the airport, I felt relieved. I called Jessie to update her on my meeting with Dr. Edward and the senator. I knew she was worried although she had said nothing.

"Hi! How did it go?" asked Jessie.

"Better than I had expected."

"Really? I can't wait to hear all about it."

"I'm on my way to the airport. I'm taking the six o'clock flight and will be there by nine-thirty. See you soon."

I had one more important call to make before I boarded the flight. At first, Billy seemed surprised to hear from me. He asked, "Is that really you, David? Honestly, I was beginning to doubt my judgment."

"No, Billy, I meant every word I said that day. And I'm calling you to confirm that, from now on, our program is strictly voluntary."

"I'm glad to hear that. Please let me know if you guys need any help in Missouri," said Billy.

With the mandatory carrier screening test dilemma settled, after reaching Calgary, the next day I embarked on something I had never done before. And this time I had to make it happen all by myself. I had promised Jessie a dinner in a beautiful restaurant on Lake Zurich, and I was going to make good on that promise on Jessie's birthday. I had exactly ten days to execute my plans.

I had already saved some money for the trip since it had to be from my personal expenses. I was hoping my savings would be enough to take care of our airfare and the hotel accommodations for a few days in the Alps. But given recent developments, I wanted to go a step further. Even if it was nothing expensive, I wanted to buy a ring for Jessie. If her answer was no, I still needed to know that. I wanted to make the gesture and propose to her properly and officially.

As I was scribbling some figures to check whether I could squeeze some extra funds for the ring from my account, Jessie walked in and asked, "What are you doing?"

Impulsively, I closed the laptop in a hurry and said, "Nothing important."

"Why are you so secretive? You're acting like you were watching porn." She paused and then suddenly asked, "Do you need money, David?"

"No. Why do you ask?"

"I don't know . . . you have some figures scribbled all over your notepad. You can tell me. I can lend you some, but I have to charge you interest though," she teased.

After that incident, naturally, I couldn't do any planning or continue my research on the ring from the office anymore. I didn't want Jessie to suspect anything. "Ten points to remember before buying your engagement ring" was informative, but I needed real help. I couldn't think of any close friend I could call to assist me with that, but I remembered two ladies who would love to help: my mother and Mrs. James.

But when I told my mother in the evening that I needed her help, she asked, "Don't you think you should take Jessie to choose the ring?"

"Then where is the surprise?" I asked.

"You never told me you wanted it to be a surprise," complained my mother.

"Well, I'm planning to take her to Zurich next weekend. If all goes well, I intend to propose to her on that Saturday evening, on her birthday. And after that, I have planned a three-day getaway to a resort in the Alps."

"Sounds like a perfect plan. I'm sure she won't suspect anything."

"I hope so. You get the ring by early next week, and I'll get the bookings done. By the way, how much will the ring cost me?"

"What's your budget?"

"That's the thing, I didn't budget for this at all. Previously, my plan was just the trip, and I've got that covered. But recently, I have been thinking maybe now is as good a time as any. Why wait?"

My mother said, "Exactly. You're doing the right thing."

"I don't know about that, Mom, but can you work with a budget of ten grand?"

"Of course, son. But why don't you let me pay for the airfare if you're short of cash?"

"Never. I just want you to buy the ring for me. Agreed?"

My mother nodded. "But I'll need the ring size. Ask her mother or her sister for help." She looked happy with my decision. We hadn't had a chance to really talk during the last few months, so that night, we chatted for nearly two hours.

When I reached home, I quickly opened my laptop and bought two round-trip tickets to Zurich, booking a chalet for three nights in Murren.

I had nine more days to fine-tune the plan and make everything perfect. But I needed more help to turn this event into a momentous occasion for Jessie. *How about Mrs. James?*

Could she be of some help? I had to contact her anyway to get the ring size. Thus, the next day, I slipped out of the office and went to meet Mrs. James. I didn't want Jessie to suspect anything.

Mrs. James hugged me as soon as she heard the whole plan. She said, "Of course, son. Consider it done. Meet me here tomorrow, and I'll pass you one of her rings."

"I need another favor, ma'am"

"Name it."

"If she says 'yes,' I want to surprise her with wishes from her friends and relatives. But the thing is, I can't be seen calling or sending text messages. I'll send one short text to you, maybe as short as the letter Y for yes. You just forward that to Lucy and to my mother. Lucy will notify Melissa. Together, they can create a chain reaction. Lucy will Tweet the news and Melissa will spread it among our contacts. I want the calls to keep coming. Jessie will love that."

"Don't worry, we got this," assured Mrs. James.

I remembered I couldn't sleep that night and a few more nights after that. I was excited and scared, too. I guess that's exactly what life was all about. Life throws hopes and disappointments. Sometimes we win, sometimes we lose. But living isn't about winning or losing; it's about the magic that unfolds every moment in front of our eyes. No one can predict with any degree of certainty what's going to happen the next day, or say, in the next minute. It's all unknown, and that's what makes living the next moment, the next day, and the next year worth it—waiting for the next abracadabra moment.

I had one last thing to do, one last person to see before I embarked on a life-changing journey. Over the last few months, I had realized we actually lived in two worlds: the one that we see when we open our eyes, the sun, the moon, the stars, and the faraway galaxies all included—one that's infinite, always a mystery, always a puzzle, always unknown. But there's also another world—one that's our very own, our individual world—made up of me and my people. If I laugh, they laugh; when I cry, they cry, too. There, happiness doesn't necessarily mean good health and wealth. One may be happy by simply looking at someone's face, making her smile, or bringing joy to her. It's difficult to explain, but it creates a chemical reaction in our brain. And that someone in my life was Jessie.

While the fear of the HD onset wasn't going to go away, I was beginning to learn to live with that. I decided to take the plunge.

Our flight was in the evening. So, instead of going to the office on Friday morning, I headed for the hospital to see Dr. Tyler.

But Dr. Tyler wasn't in his room. Alice told me he would be taking two classes, back-to-back. And then he was scheduled for surgery on a cardiac patient.

"You can catch him in-between the two classes if it's something urgent. Otherwise, you can come back in the evening," said Alice.

But I couldn't wait until the evening. I might miss my flight if I tried that, so I thanked Alice and walked toward the university. Naturally, I took the shortest route through the Hall of Fame. But as I walked past those photographs once again, I suddenly stopped at one of their new additions. I couldn't believe my eyes. *How did our voluntary carrier screening test poster for parental fitness make its way up there? There must have been some kind of mistake.* It read, "Revolution in healing begins with a revolution in thinking." I was stunned. I was dying to know the truth. I quickened my pace.

I reached the lecture hall even before Dr. Tyler finished his first class, and I waited outside. He was quite surprised to see me there. He said, "Hi David! What are you doing here?"

"I wanted to talk to you, sir. I have something very important to tell you."

"Well then, walk with me. I have another class now. Or you can come back to my room in the evening."

"That's the thing, sir. I'm flying off to Zurich with Jessie this evening. I'm going to propose to her there, and I wanted your blessing."

"Good luck, son. You know you always have my blessing."

"I know that, sir, and thank you." I had about two more minutes before we reached Dr. Tyler's second classroom. I asked, "Do you know anything about the carrier screening test poster in the Hall of Fame, sir?" My understanding was nothing significant happened in that hospital without Dr. Tyler's knowledge.

He said, "I thought your boss, Dr. Edward, must have told you."

"Told me what, sir?"

"That he called and told me how you convinced them to keep the tests strictly voluntary. I'm very proud of you, son. And since it's a voluntary program now, Christchurch hospital can also take part in your 'carrier screening test' awareness campaign."

"That's great news, sir. Thank you."

"I didn't do anything, son. It's all you. It's your program that's in the Hall of Fame. The admin office asked for my permission, and I saw no reason to disappoint them. The solution was right there in front of us, but just having a carrier screening test wasn't enough—educating people about it will now complete the circle. You have totally revitalized the old carrier screening test with an active awareness campaign. You discovered the missing link. We're all very proud of you in this hospital."

He extended his right hand, smiled, and said, "All the best, son." Then he disappeared behind the closed door.

I stood outside the door, dazed for I don't remember how long. When I got my senses back, I took a slow walk to the small park opposite the hospital building. I remembered how, nearly two years before, I had sat exactly on the same bench after I'd been told I was HD positive. That day, I had thought my life was over. But two years later, when technically, I was closer to my HD onset, surprisingly, I felt better. I felt alive. In the last two years, I had discovered a new path to the future, I had made more friends than I could ever imagine in my lifetime, and I had found love.

I took the ring out of my pocket—I had just collected it from my mother that morning—and held it tightly in my hands. I was no expert in engagement rings, but it looked great to me. *If all goes as planned, within the next forty-eight hours, I will be starting a new life with Jessie.*

I looked at the hospital building in front, but this time, I didn't feel sad. I pictured new milestones ahead of me: our engagement, our life together, canvassing for carrier screening and getting more signatures for voluntary parental fitness tests. Jessie and I had crossed several milestones together. I would never forget the day when Jessie first told me about testing the parents for their fitness, the day she got all excited and called me in the supermarket to tell me we had two hundred and thirty-one hits in a day. True, we didn't count hits for very long, but looking back, those were important moments. We cherished every new comment and all new participants as the voluntary carrier screening test signatures for parental fitness were mounting up. The day I first uploaded my "unfit" certificate, I had no idea one day it could touch millions. People from all over the world rushed in to disclose their genetic diseases with one goal in mind: a safer next generation.

The best part was that, while all this was happening in the gigantic cosmic world, in my own universe, I had found someone special: my soulmate. The all-important health and wealth in the outside world became nothing to me. I didn't care about the HD anymore. *So what if I am dying; aren't we all going to die, anyway?* I was dying to love and be loved.

About the Author

Uday Mukerji was born in India and had worked as a creative director in advertising agencies in Singapore for nearly twenty years. He started his carrier as a copywriter and soon moved up to assume bigger responsibilities. While working on various advertising campaigns was great fun, in 2009, he decided to change gear and pursue a career in writing.

His first literary fiction – a 2017 Readers' Favorite Award Winner – Love, Life, and Logic was published by Harvard Square Editions, NY in November 2016.

www.ingramcontent.com/pod-product-compliance
Lightning Source LLC
Chambersburg PA
CBHW021436020726
47499CB00006BA/2026